MUSTANG
Wild Spirit of the West

THE MARGUERITE HENRY HORSESHOE LIBRARY

Misty of Chincoteague

King of the Wind

Sea Star, Orphan of Chincoteague

Born to Trot

Brighty of the Grand Canyon

Justin Morgan Had a Horse

Black Gold

Stormy, Misty's Foal

Mustang, Wild Spirit of the West

MUSTANG

Wild Spirit of the West

By MARGUERITE HENRY

Illustrated by Robert Lougheed

CHECKERBOARD PRESS

NEW YORK

The quotation on page 81 is from *Cowboys and Indians*, by Kathryn and Byron Jackson, © copyright 1948 by Golden Press.

The quotation on page 86 is from *Prayers from the Ark*, by Carmen Bernos de Gasztold, translated from the French by Rumer Godden. Copyright 1962 by Rumer Godden; published by Viking Press.

Dedicated to
"Wild Horse Annie"
in whose moccasins
I have been walking
these many moons

Contents

1. Saved by a Mustang 11

2. Pa's Pardner 21

3. Every Bad Has a Good 32

4. Trapped! 39

5. "To Lazy Heart Ranch" 47

6. It Takes a Smart Mustang— 55

7. Operation Rescue 66

8. Our Small Happy World 73

9. More Dead than Alive 82

10. Mice and Mustangs 90

11. The Scales Tip Even 97

12. The New Challenge 108

13. *The Mustang Bill*   116

14. *Failure at Fernley*   126

15. *"Wild Horse Annie"*   134

16. *Stockings Hung by the Fire*   142

17. *At Black Rock Desert*   150

18. *Found—a Champion*   161

19. *The Power of Children*   166

20. *A Growing Storm*   173

21. *No Compromise!*   180

22. *A Call from Washington*   187

23. *In the Witness Seat*   197

24. *"We the People—"*   203

    Roaming Free   221

MUSTANG

Wild Spirit of the West

1. Saved by a Mustang

IF GOD has a kind of plan for all of us, I like to think He coupled me with horses right from the start. It is not just my own mustang, Hobo, that is part of me. All horses call to me. We sort of belong together. This could not be just an accident.

I remember the first time I saw a band of wild mustangs. It was only a flash. My Pa and I were freighting a load of wool over the mountains to California when suddenly he reined in and pointed. I saw the reason. Far off on a mesa a string of mustangs was running into the wind. It must have been into the wind, for their tails streamed out behind and their manes lifted like licks of flame. And just by looking I was out there with them, and I could hear their snortings and their hoofs ringing, and I could feel my own hair blowing and my lungs gulping for air, and I shivered in joy at such freedom.

I remember whispering, "Whose are they, Pa?"

And Pa saying, "They're runaways—gone wild." There was a look of wanting in Pa's face, but excitement too at the free wildness.

"Will they always live there, free like that . . . and then their colts and grand-colts?"

Pa startled me with his sudden stern tone. "They could! If men don't get too grabby for every smitch of land for their cattle."

Even as he said it, a cow bawled nearby. And in the distance a fading line of dust was all that remained of the wild ones.

Pa clucked to his team and we drove off. For miles of mountain turns we rode in silence. We were still holding onto the beauty we had seen. I could still hear the echo of faraway hoofbeats. I could listen to nothing else. Yet even as I sighed in joy I felt a vague, uneasy worry. I didn't want anything ever to happen to them; I wanted them always to be free. But could they?

That was the first time horses called to me. But now I know that God had a plan for me long before that. On clear, cold nights when the stars are all in their rightful places I know He had me in mind as long ago as that time when my Pa was just a baby and almost died on the desert. But he didn't die because . . .

"Oh, the cowards never started
And the weak ones died by the way . . ."

That's how my Grandma always began the true story of how my Pa was saved. Then she'd clear her throat, moisten her lips, and with a look of joy upon her face she'd plunge into her covered-wagon days.

"Our wagon rolled through dust. A choking, sneezy wilderness of dust . . . from nowhere to nowhere." She paused a moment, her small bright eyes remembering. She stared over my head as if the whole panorama of her pioneer days was flashing on the wall behind me. "Our four horses made furrows through it, kicking up great clouds of dust that turned the brown-coated ones to gray and the gray ones to white. Even Nelly's colt tagging along beside her was fuzzy-furred with dust, and its whiskers white like a goat's.

"Annie!" she'd say. "Your Pa couldn't of come into this world at a worser time."

"Why, Grandma?" I'd ask. Even when I got to be ten or eleven, I'd still ask "Why?" right there. And she'd say:

"Why? Because we hadn't a home, and barely enough vittles to last to California. And no money to buy more. That's why.

"How'd you like it, Annie, if one day your husband is fore-man of a big silver mine in Ione, Nevada. And you have a nice home with pretties on the what-not and red geraniums growing all over the windows, and all to once the mine closes down. Just like that!

"And the very next day," here Grandma's voice turned softer, "you bring into the world the cutest button-nosed baby ever, and hardly a bunting to wrap him in. If he'd just of waited till we got to my people in Grass Valley . . . "

"But he didn't!" I crowed. "And I'm glad, because then there wouldn't be any story. Go on, Grandma. Go on!"

Grandma's eyes narrowed and her jaw muscles tightened. "The reason we hadn't any money was because that scalawag of a mine-owner skips off to San Francisco. He promises to come back with a big roll of money, enough to pay off the miners. But what does he do?"

"*He never comes back!*" I filled in.

"And what does your dear sweet crazy Grandpa do?"

Here I always waited for Grandma to blow up with pride.

"He parcels out all his own money so the miners could buy wagons and light out for greener pastures And they did. Mean-while, we wait weeks and weeks while our little village turns into a ghost town. Then we have to leave, too. We decide to go to Grass Valley, California, where my folks lived. That last morning I watered my geraniums just like always and pinched off the dead ones. Your Grandpa hooked up our four mustangs that he had caught and gentled, and off we went in the wagon that I'd roofed over with our bedsheets."

"Were there only *four* mustangs?"

Grandma's eyes came to mine and smiled. "Besides the leaders and wheelers there was a skinny little colt tagging along free. He'd make little forays of his own and then come kiting back to Nelly." Grandma stroked my head now as if I was a colt, and she talked fast to get to the miracle.

"Nelly's colt and my baby, who is now your Pa, were born at almost the same hour. Your Grandpa was so busy running betwixt her and me I wondered which mattered more, and when both babies were safely born he was nigh as proud of Nelly's

colt as of his own son. Seems the colt had some Arabian or Andalusian blood in him that set him off as something special.

"Well, like I said, we hooked up our mustangs and started off, the colt trailing along. A few days later we run out of water. Everywhere we look there's nothing but dust and rocks and sand and dust and dust and dust. Sometimes we'd ride all day without seeing anything else. When we come to water, it's more like soapsuds, and I try to drink it, but it won't go down. And my milk for Baby Joe dries up. But Nelly is smarter. She eats any old rabbit brush or sagebrush, and her milk runs free and she nurses her colt, but I can't nurse my baby."

My eyes were fixed on Grandma's. "Then what?"

"My baby yelled at first, hour after hour. Then he whimpered. And in no time it seemed he got all shriveled looking, like a little old man. One day your Grandpa says, 'There ain't no other way. Nelly's got to be Baby Joe's nurser.' And he milked Nelly and we spooned her milk into the baby's mouth, a slow drop at a time."

The miracle held us both in a web of stillness. I imagined I was right there, helping to milk Nelly, and spoon-feeding Grandma's baby, who was my Pa.

"Your Grandpa was glad Baby Joe was saved. But a few days later a misery came over him when he told me he had to kill Nelly's colt. 'I got to do it,' he said, his eyes full of hurt. 'She ain't got enough milk for two.' Oh, Annie, it hurt him so. He'd rather of shot off his right arm. 'I'll just wait till morning,' he said, 'and then I'll do it. Painless as I can.' "

"Then what?"

16

"The wind woke us up next morning, tearing at our wagon flaps. When we looked out, all our horses were gone! Nothing left but hoofprints circling the camp, making off in all directions like the spokes of a wheel.

"Your Grandpa howled like a savage. 'Injuns done it!' he yelled. 'Only Injuns could thieve so quiet.' He buckled on his cartridge belt, a wild look in his eye.

"He was right. Almost at once three young Paiutes appeared out of the brush. Their faces were smeared with green and red paint, and their heads decked out in crow feathers. They were riding scrawny cayuses. It was plain to see why our stout horses were worth the stealing.

" 'Grub!' the oldest one muttered. He pointed at our wagon traces, showing he was ready to trade for our missing team.

"Pa's hand reached for his gun; it was all I could do to stop him. Then I ran for the wagon and brought out little Joe. He made pitiful cries of hunger and he seemed all mouth, like a baby bird. I made sign talk to the Indians . . . how my baby would die if they didn't bring Nelly back.

"The oldest one grinned. 'What you give?'

" 'You find our horses first,' your Grandpa threatened. 'Bring all back. Then we parley. We make gifts.'

"They left as silently as they came. Meanwhile I prayed and hugged the baby, and your Grandpa paced in fury around the wagon, his rifle held in front of him. After what seemed a long time the Paiutes came back, leading our four mustangs, three of them willing, but Nelly a-balkin' and a-whinnerin' for her colt. This time the faces of the Indians were grim.

"The oldest one brandished a knife. 'Great Spirit tells Injuns keep little one,' he grunted. 'He make good pony. What you give for big ones?'

"Grandpa brought out a side of bacon. The Paiute shook his head. He poked inside the wagon and pointed at the three sacks of flour and the lone sack of sugar. He held up two fingers and then one. And so your Grandpa added two sacks of flour and our only sack of sugar to the side of bacon. Then the Indians rode off gruntin' and happy."

"And Grandpa never had to kill the colt," I sighed in relief. "He probably grew up to be a fine Indian pony."

"I'm sure of it," Grandma nodded. "And with our four mustangs we traveled all the way to California. Your Grandpa and me had mighty slim rations. But Baby Joe fattened up on mare's milk."

I wanted the story never to end. I tried to string it out. "Grandma!" I cried. "Did you find your folks? And what was Grass Valley like?"

"Oh, it was a sightful! Grass green as Heaven, and arms flung wide in welcome, and my own Papa proud as a punkin over Baby Joe, but happier-seeming about the mustangs. You see, he needed extra horses in his hauling business. But it was my Mamma who seemed happiest of all. She held the baby close to her, making little clucking noises. 'Land-a-mercy,' she purred to him, 'your family is a puny-looking outfit. But you,' she said, kissing him soundly, 'you got cheeks round and rosy as our pippins. And to think you was saved by the milk of a mustang.'"

2. Pa's Pardner

AND SO my Pa didn't die. He had a big life to live, and that included me.

I don't remember my father clearly until I was a husky three-year-old and we were living on the outskirts of Reno. He was a tall, commanding man with dark hair and high cheekbones like the Paiute Indians. But his eyes were blue, bright steel blue, and so deep-set I thought they went clear through to the back of his head. His business was freighting goods by horse and wagon across the mountains. It was called The Mustang Express. It took him away from home for days at a time. When he was gone, I always pictured him on a pedestal right up there in the mountains, big as God and Moses.

Well, that day when I "met" Pa, he swung me aboard Hobo, a young buckskin colt with a blazed face and black mane and tail. For a few moments I was riding high. Then my two little boy-cousins came running up, begging to join me; and Pa, always eager to oblige, hefted them up, too.

Hobo hadn't been broke to ride three bouncing kids sitting clear back to his hip bones. He humped up like a cat, made one winding jump skyward, and tossed us high. Pa caught my cousins, but he had only two hands; so I landed in front of Hobo's feet, sitting on my breeches—cushioned by diapers, I'm ashamed to admit.

Hobo nosed me all over as if in apology, and Pa did the same. Then he sent my crying cousins into the house and came back to me. As soon as he'd dusted me off, he held me at arm's length and looked at me hard, eye to eye.

"Pardner!" he said. Then he gulped like he was choking on a chicken bone. He tried again. "Pardner!" he said. "I'm the one who's to fault. Hobo's gentle as a lamb, only he can't get used to anybody in the rear seat. Even when I lay his saddle-blanket too far hindwards, he lets me know. Now I'm going to put you right back up. You sit chilly as a dead Indian and he'll step along careful like you were a setting hen with a whole nestful of eggs."

Before I could make an outcry, there I was riding high again. Pa showed me how to hang on by holding two fistfuls of mane. It was almost like having reins! Then he tapped Hobo on the rump. And oh glory, Hobo stepped out brisk as though he was heading for oats. Pa had to run to keep up, but he didn't hold onto me! Little as I was, I knew I belonged up there. I felt big and important and supremely happy. I heard myself whooping it up like the cowboys. If I live to be a hundred and three, I'll never forget my first ride on Hobo.

Too soon it was over, and Papa set me down outside the corral. Then from his great height he reached over and shook hands. I remember just how it felt—my stubby fingers almost lost in his big calloused palm. But I squeezed back, hard. And that's when I knew my name was "Pardner." All through school I insisted on spelling it that way. Teachers could be wrong, but not Papa.

Besides being a freighter, Pa was a mustanger. In those days the wild horses roaming the hills belonged to anyone. Mustangin' was an honorable profession, with the horses given a fighting chance to escape. Pa and my uncle would ride into the foothills where the mustangs hid. They'd sight a herd, and playing the wind right they'd drive them into a box canyon, rope one apiece, and free the rest.

Most times Pa'd come home with only two wild ones to be gentled. Sometimes with none. And sometimes he would make a trade with the Paiutes and then he'd come home with a whole string of half-broke mustangs. "Broomtails" the men called them.

But to me they were unearthly beautiful, as if God had put a special touch on them. I was fascinated by their eye-lights. It seemed a fire burned inside 'em, a fire that glowed warm and brown-red for quiet-spoken people, but a fire that could rage and destroy if it had a mind to. Since Pa and I were

pardners, he said the horses belonged to me as much as to him.

He never came home from his long trips without some extra surprise for me, maybe a pair of beaded moccasins or a baby lizard. Once it was a "bummer" lamb. In case you don't know, a bummer is a twin whose mother won't nurse it and it takes to bumming milk from other ewes. Sheepmen are glad to give it away. For weeks I bottle-fed that bummer until it got to butting me whenever it was hungry. I felt exactly like a ewe-mother, and I could see why they were anxious to let their youngsters go to grass.

My Pa, with his deep thoughtful eyes, understood that some children are babies until they're ten or more, and some are just naturally born old. I was grown up at five. That's what I thought, and so did he. He expected me to sleep with my boots handy and respond to his whistle like a fireman.

My main job was grooming. Pa liked his teams to look smart when they hauled a load. So early each morning before the sun topped over the mountains, I'd be standing up on a box, brushing like all get-out. The horses would lower their heads for me to comb their forelocks and they'd let me wipe out the corners of their eyes, and even the dust from their

nostrils. When their tails were tangled with tiny thorns, Pa'd pour Nunn's oil on them, and then I could slide the prickly things down the long hairs until that matted mess became a pretty good-looking tail.

Mom put up with my being more boy than girl because she thought it wouldn't last. Only one thing she balked at, and that was my visiting the cabins out back where the teamsters and their womenfolk lived. She almost put a stop to it, especially the night I tore home screaming hysterically.

I can remember the evening. It was too early for lamplight. Mount Rose seemed very near, and purple-blue with sunset. One of the teamsters' wives had invited me to come over for dessert. Cooking was her hobby. She often made chocolate angel pie topped with clouds of whipped cream, and she stuffed dates with pecan meats and rolled them in sugar—even when it wasn't Thanksgiving or Christmas. This night it was a deep dish cobbler of black Bing cherries. After I gobbled it, I chattered on and on until she dropped off to sleep. Feeling hurt, I washed my pie plate and was about to tiptoe for home when a voice outside broke the stillness.

"Yep, fellers, this here yarn is about Injun trickery."

With my ears asking, What? What? I joined the men who were sitting on the stoop. They took no more notice of me than if I'd been a cricket.

"Nevada was wild country then," the old teamster was saying. He balled a wad of tobacco into his cheek, and he chawed and spat before he went on. "This white settler, he liked to hunt and he needed a good trackin' dog. Well, he meets up with a Injun who's got a red-bone hound, and he figgered here's a fine workin' dog. So he offers the Injun a teensy poke of gold.

"The Injun shakes his head to show 'tain't enough. So the

hunter, he adds a pinch more of gold, and then another, and this goes on and on until the poke is dang-near full.

"The feller's disgusted and just about to call the whole deal off when the Injun ties a rope to the hound, tests to see it's snug, and with a funny grin hands the rope over.

"So the buyer, he ties it to the tailgate of his wagon and goes on his way. And would you b'lieve it, less'n half a mile down the road a stranger shouts at him, 'Hey, feller, yer dawg's got free.'

"Sure enough! That hound was flying back to the Injun like an arrow. And you know how the hunter got his revenge for that tricky knot the Injun tied?"

"No. How?" we all cried in chorus.

"Quicker than you could bat an eye, he grabs his rifle and shoots the hound dead."

Stunned, I stumbled over the men's feet, running down the steps, screaming for home. I burst into the house, gasping out the whole story.

When I stopped for breath, Pa said, "Yes, that was mighty bad, Pardner. Only one thing could of made it worse."

"What?" I asked, choking on my tears and the heart gone out of me.

"Torture. The killin' bullet came so fast it didn't hurt that hound. But it hurt the hunter aplenty. Maybe not at first, but to my notion it grew to be a festerin' sore. And it hurt the Indian, too. He must of felt pretty mean when he found his old huntin' companion dead." Pa's eyes slitted until I could see only the black holes. "But it was quick and clean. The one thing I can't abide is a killer who tortures his creatures."

For days after that I didn't go back to the cabins. But at last I couldn't resist the magic talk, and the cowboy songs, and the lovely desserts. Mom thought I picked up my swear words there, but I really didn't. Pa had much better ones, like "Goshallhimlock" and "Dummitdell," and he knew how to whistle them through the wide space in his front teeth so they made a grand scary sound, like a bullwhip. I used to practice them under Grandma's and my bed when no one else was in the house.

Before I get on to that big plan God had in mind for me, and how He always coupled me with horses, I must tell you about our family.

I shared my room with Grandma. She went out nursing by the day and wasn't at home much. So I got to practice my swearing pretty often. I loved Grandma and was never afraid of her, even though she stood six feet in her white nurse shoes, and wore a high starched collar that made her look tall as a Spanish queen.

With Grandma, and Mom and Pa, and Pa's sister, Aunt Elvira, to love and protect me, I knew that life was good. Even as a little girl of five, I knew it, but I didn't know then *how* good it was. Sitting in the grass, shoulder-to-shoulder with the bummer lamb, and the stay-at-home horses putting their noses together and bowing their heads over us, and the sun going down behind the mountains, I can remember shivering with a tingly happiness I can't explain. Maybe I felt akin to all four-legged folk who don't need words to show their content.

The bummer and the horses were good listeners, and I'd make up stories to tell them, just like I was their mother. My favorite big whopper was realer than real. I told how Pa asked me one day to go mustangin' with him, and we went up into the Pine Nut Mountains and on a high mesa there was a band of horses, not a big band, just a little one, but extra wild and beautiful. We were about to rope one when a gust of wind hit us. Like a voice in the wind I heard:

> *The mountains are mine,*
> *and all the creatures in it,*

and I knew it was the voice of Godamighty.

Pa'd be coming home then and I'd have to excuse myself from the critters to go to meet him. I guess I had a time-clock in my head the way horses do, for I'd know just when Pa would be coming and where he'd expect me to be, right at the edge of town. When he saw me, he'd swoop me up as if I were no bigger'n a dropped handkerchief and plop me on Hobo or Old Baldy, and I'd ride bareback all the way to the barn. Then, alone, I'd lead each horse to the watering trough. The other teamsters would let me do the same thing for their horses. For an hour or so I was the busiest teamster of them all, and I believed in my heart that the horses were just as eager to come home to *me* as to their barley suppers.

Even the washing up for my own supper was fun because of the crazy mirror tacked on the side of the barn. It had a jagged crack as though lightning had struck it. So after washing in the tin basin with the yellow see-through soap, I'd stand up on the bench to dry my face and to laugh at myself. It was like going to the mirror-house in the amusement park. One half of your face set up higher than the other half. And I'd make faces and laugh until I had to give up my place to Pa or one of the teamsters who didn't think it was nearly so funny They soused their heads in the sudsy water and combed without even looking in the mirror. I didn't blame 'em for not looking; some of them were pretty ugly.

At night with the moon-shadows playing across my bed, I'd drop off to sleep almost before my head hit the pillow. And I'd dream of a barn with roomy box stalls for the horses, but one horse was all my own and he would be looking for me over the half-door, nickering for me. Just me.

3. *Every Bad Has a Good*

WELL, ONE night when I was five-and-a-half I didn't fall asleep at pillow's touch. I had a queer floating feeling as if I'd been shot from a cannon way out into space and couldn't get back. Yet I could hear voices on earth, dear familiar ones.

"You'll see, Joe," Mom was saying. . . .

Right here I've got to interrupt and tell you more about Mom. She was so good and pretty that I hardly ever thought about her. She didn't need my help the way Pa did. She had Grandma and Aunt Elvira to help her, and things in the kitchen always happened on time. Meals came regular. So I didn't even think about them in my hurry to get back out with the horses where I was needed.

Well, on this night Mom was saying, "You'll see, Joe, Annie'll outgrow her horse-fever. I remember my own tomboy days—I wanted to be a high trapeze star, and look at me now. Happy as a chickadee with one little tyke to care for and another on the way, and I'm praying for a boy."

Another baby? A real boy? Even in my dizzy outer-world feeling I hated the news. I didn't want a brother to take my place and to be Pa's Pardner. But Pa made it all right again. He talked about me.

"I don't think she'll ever outgrow horses," he said. "I've seen her with 'em, her feelin's exposed like raw wounds. She's terrified when they are. She'll stand alongside 'em, blinded by lightning, battered by wind. When one's sufferin' and in pain, it's like it was her pain. And when they're friskin' and happy, she's happy."

I didn't mean to listen, but I was too fascinated not to. Besides, it was true!

"Mebbe," Pa was saying, "when she grows up she'll be a doctor for horses, or something big like that. Mebbe her hankerin' to go with me on every trip and her adoptin' each wild'un I bring in is all part of a big plan."

"Like what?" came Mom's voice.

"Don't know. I just figger it's some special kind of learnin' she's getting. God's sure trainin' her different from most girls."

I must have fallen asleep then. When I awoke, I was screaming in pain. It was the next afternoon or maybe the next after that, for the sun was coming in the west window, and there, sitting on the edge of my bed, was good old Dr. Whitcomb with his white dusty hair and his black rusty suit. He was trying to move my head, and Mom with her hand clamped over her mouth and Grandma in her starched nurse's uniform and Aunt Elvira with her big teeth gritted were all standing by looking fit to cry. And I not caring if they did, for I was hurting from the top of my head all the way down to my tailbone. In the midst of my screaming I saw my Pa in the doorway, and I stopped the way you turn off a spigot. He looked years older than yesterday, and his face was gray as gray and his eyes sunk deep in his head.

Dr. Whitcomb let go of my neck. Then in the stillness he said, "I think, though we can't be sure, it's the polio."

From that day till I was eleven, I had pains all up and down my spine. I'm going to skip over those sickness years fast as I can, because now I wear blinders on my memory so I won't even think about them. But if I skipped them entirely, you'd never understand why I had to do what I did when the time came.

Besides, every bad has a good. I really got to know my Grandma. Mom, of course, was busy with my new baby brother. But Grandma stopped being a nurse for strangers, and she gave all her time to me. Her swirly, weepy-willow skirts were a refuge in pain. And her spirit was strong enough to lift and hold me.

Each morning after she helped me out of bed and dressed me, we walked the three blocks to a new doctor in town, who worked on my spine and neck with his bare hands. We had to walk there instead of ride because I couldn't stand the slightest jarring; it made the pinched nerves send out needles of pain. We must have been a queer sight—big, towering Grandma taking little mincing steps to match my painful slow ones. It took us a full hour, going and coming every day, week after week.

In the doctor's office my swearing stood me in good stead. The doctor, who was a red-haired young man with a voice like a bassoon, never seemed shocked at all. He said to Grandma,

"Mrs. Bronn, I couldn't work on Annie and manipulate her muscles, I just couldn't hurt her like this if she cried like a child. But she's taking it like a man, and talking like a man helps her. Some day she'll walk right out of this office, square and firm."

It was funny what silly things the young doctor bribed me with—Kewpie dolls and tea sets made of tin, and other things I couldn't use. But Grandma knew what I needed. She bought me shiny red shoes she couldn't afford, while she wore cardboard in the soles of hers. And she read me books bursting with adventure. Oh, how I ate and breathed and slept with them. Some we read twenty-six times. And they were all living inside of me until I was fit to burst.

Now books were my life. For these moments I skimmed across the ice with Hans Brinker, I wrassled wildcats with Daniel Boone, I climbed mountains with Heidi, and it was *my* thumb instead of Peter's that plugged the hole in the dike!

That same doctor sent me to school in an agony of braces. It wasn't that they hurt me; it was the awful fun-making of my schoolmates. "Hey, Annie, how come *you* get excused from

gym?" "Lucky you ain't a horse or your Pa'd shoot you for going gimpy."

I hated standing on the sidelines, watching the other kids doing the things I wanted to do, and trying to let their cruel teasing slide off the hard shell I was growing.

But what happened at school was as nothing compared to my separation from the horses. I couldn't ride them, or hook up for Pa, or even brush them. And the way my Pa acted was even worse. He moved about me in a sort of tight quietness, stepping careful and awkward, just the way I did. It was like *his* back was twisted, too. And he never called me "Pard" any more. He called me "Annie," through lips that hardly opened.

Even so, I wanted oh so much to live, and I dreamed of a time when I'd be well, and of the ranch I'd own and the horses I'd ride. Mostly I'd dream of that special horse who would whinner for me over the half-door of his stall. The dreams were fiercely real because they took the place of riding and skating and jumping rope.

All this while Grandma was my salvation. She rummaged around in her memory and came up with exciting true stories of pioneer days. Over and over I asked for the story of how the mustang mare saved Pa's life. And she taught me how to knit and to sew, and to make my own dresses. Always we chose the brightest colors. Sometimes I was a redbird. Sometimes a bluejay. And she taught me to be expert at tiddledy-winks and jacks and marbles so I could beat my boy cousins.

She even taught me to cook. Floating island pudding was my triumph. This meant I had to gather the eggs. In careful, halty steps I went into the chicken house, and except for one grumpy old hen, they let me reach in under them and take their eggs while they were still warm.

One·day I came across a hen on a hidden nest in the hay mow. I didn't know she'd been setting there for three weeks. With a loud squawk, she surrendered one brown egg. I was already late for school; so I tucked it into my pocket. All morning long I sat in the hot schoolroom unmindful of the egg. At recess I fell into a puddle, and my teacher helped me back into the room and sat me on the radiator to dry off. That night while I was doing my lessons in front of our big red-bellied stove, I heard the faintest "peep" from my pocket. The baby chick had hatched right there!

Pa looked over his newspaper at the scrawny little life in my hand. A smile of pride spread across his face. "Your walking so gentle and careful, Annie, it could only of happened to you," he said.

For a long time I believed that yellow fluff of a chick was part of God's way of making it up to me.

4. *Trapped!*

GRADUALLY, WHEN I was nearly eleven, the hurting eased, but I still walked slowly and carried my head sidewise, for my spine hadn't straightened. And I still couldn't ride or jump rope or play run-my-good-sheep run.

Pa and Mom wanted to do everything they could to help me. So one spring day, just after school let out, I was bundled off to a hospital in San Francisco where crippled children were treated without any cost to their parents. The only thing the parents had to promise was not to come to visit for several months, as it might slow the recovery.

"You'll like it there," Mom had said. "There'll be other

children like you. And sooner than soon you'll be home again."

But I didn't like it. And there weren't other children like me. The others wore casts or braces on an arm or a leg, and they could race down the halls on crutches. But I was in jail. A surgeon locked me up in a plaster cast. It began at my hips and went up and up until it covered even the top of my head. I looked like a humpty-dumpty with skinny arms and legs dangling. Holes were cut for my mouth, my eyes and ears, and a little hole was left at the top so I could scratch my head with the blunt end of Grandma's knitting needles, which she had sent along to keep my hands busy.

At first I didn't mind the cage much because I was excited by the prospect of emerging tall and straight and beautiful. But soon I began to feel smothered. My prison was crushing me. It seemed as if my spirit was battering against the cast, like a moth beating its wings in a glass jar. In the dark of night I would fill my lungs to bursting, hoping to crack the cast and escape to freedom. When this failed, I tried to claw it open with my fingernails. But it was strong as steel. I was like an animal in a trap, all crazy from hurt and fear. I prayed to God to set me free, crooked or lame.

But I didn't know if He was hearing me, and I'd sob myself to sleep, dreaming of our house, and Hobo rubbing off his winter hair and snortin' in that friendly way, and sometimes I'd be feeding the bummer lamb and him buttin' sassy-like if I didn't hold the bottle just so. Then I'd wake up in the dark, and the house was not there, or Hobo, or the corral, or the cabins out back. Or Pa and Mom. Or Grandma.

While I couldn't have visitors, I could have letters. But somehow when they came, they made me all the sadder. I missed out on so many things—Hobo's helping to break a new mustang to harness, my little brother's new puppy dog, and Aunt Elvira's wedding. She sent me a piece of the cake to sleep on and a picture of her in her wedding dress. She was pretty in white; it made her teeth look smaller. I slept with the cake under my pillow for two nights and then ate it. It made me feel more lost and lonesome than before.

Even Grandma's letters broke my heart. She had a full-time job now, working in a hospital. "It's a sit-down job at the admissions desk," she wrote. "I live here nights, too." At this I blubbered all down the inside of my cast. How could I picture my bed at home without the big flannel warmth of Grandma!

A dozen times a day I looked at Mom's watch that she had given me as a parting gift. "Every time you look at it," she'd said, "you'll know what we're doing at home and that we're thinking of you. It'll hurry the time along."

But nothing could hurry those poky hands. They lagged and dragged, not trying to get ahead at all.

The only bright spot in my life was a large painting in the hall that I had to pass on the way to the bathroom. I would glance at it hurriedly going, and stop to worship it for a long time a-coming back. The painting, called "Roaming Free," showed a band of wild horses skimming across the desert, manes and tails flowing. The exciting thing was that they were leaping right out of the picture, at me! And they were strong and wild and muscley as if they'd found good grass and good water and lived a good life. If ever I went a-mustangin' with my Pa, that's the kind I'd like to catch, especially that little buckskin in front.

The picture had me bewitched. It was as if someone had taken my dream, and by mouth-to-mouth breathing had brought it alive. I studied it with all my senses. I could just feel what it was like out there, winging along with the herd. "I hope they never catch you, little Buck," I'd say under my breath. "Go it, you little bullet! Go it!"

I gloried in his freedom, but at the same time I wanted to capture him, too. I wanted to be a mustanger now that I was a grown-up eleven. I could see the chase in my mind and feel it in my heart. I could even smell the desert. And there was Pa on Old Baldy and me on Hobo galloping over sand and sage and rock, and we'd flush the bunch of wild ones out of the foot-hills, and we'd cut little Buck away from the others. Riding herd on him, we'd run him into a box canyon and I'd capture him! Alone! He'd be mine! Mine to gentle and . . .

I felt a hand on my arm! I jumped, startled out of my trance. "I like that picture too, Annie." It was my doctor. I hated him because he was my jailer. His hair was black and curly, and I could see horns coming up out of the kinky places, just like they were there.

"Wild horses aren't really wild, Annie, you know. They're *feral*," he said in a voice so tender I was surprised. It wasn't his doctor-voice at all. "Do you know, my child, what feral means?"

I didn't answer. I clamped my lips tight; I wasn't going to show my ignorance to him.

"Well, feral means gone wild. Those free-roaming horses are offspring of tame horses. Years ago they probably escaped from missions, or Indian camps, or ranches, and then they multiplied like weeds. In fact, you might say a mustang is a kind of weed."

"A weed!" I repeated in disgust. "You should see my Hobo!"

"There, there, Annie. It's like some garden flowers—like the larkspur and lilies. In the east, they jump the walls and go wild. Some people think they're regular weeds, not having the eyes to see. It's the same with horses. Weedlike though they be, a band of mustangs racing across the sand under the pale desert sky is one of the finest sights in the West."

My hate began to melt. "Then you know all about this picture, don't you? Who put it there?" I asked.

"I did," he replied quietly. "I felt the artist understood the beauty and wild freedom of the mustangs. And sometimes when I feel all tired and trapped . . ."

"You? Trapped?" I stammered almost angrily, seeing him standing there, his big arm muscles bulging.

He shut his eyes and sighed. And when he spoke, his voice was gentle and sad. "Do you think," he asked softly, "a man is free who has to put little girls in plaster casts, knowing how it feels inside? Do you think that a doctor who must treat sickness he cannot cure, and dying people he cannot save, is really free? It's the worst kind of prison of all. You do your best, you pray, you beat against the bars. But sometimes— many times—you lose every step of the way. You are trapped and helpless. Do you know what I mean?"

I nodded dumbly with tears in my throat. But a thrill ran

up and down my crooked spine as I felt a glow of kinship with the doctor. He shared my prison!

"So," he said, "I look long and deep at the painting until my tiredness goes away and something inside me is all free once more, like the mustangs tearing down the wind. Do you understand, Annie?"

I just nodded again, being too choked up for talking.

"That's why I had the painting hung there," the doctor said. "I thought maybe the mustangs could help the patients, too, when they felt tired and trapped like me."

The tears came up from my throat and moved to my eyes, and then rolled down inside my cast. But I was crying from happiness, knowing I wasn't alone any more.

The big doctor turned and walked away. And I could see that his shoulders were heavy and bent with his worry.

It was that picture in the hospital which saw me through. Sometime I would be free like that. All those days I lived on the promise of my own liberty.

Weeks went by. And months. Spring came again, and with it my freedom. Early one morning the cast was taken off entirely. I could bend! I could run! Soon I could ride Hobo!

I rushed to the mirror to see the transformation. One look and I gaped in horror. The face that stared back at me was the one I had seen long ago in the cracked mirror on the barn. The two sides of my face did not match! The hard plaster cast had made it grow crooked.

This time I did not laugh. I hid my face in shame and sobbed. All that day I felt abandoned by the world. Naked and despised, as if God cared more about poor fallen sparrows than me. I heard the nurses whispering behind my back. "Whatever is to become of the poor child now?" For a moment I longed to run to the hospital dump and find the discarded cast, and shut myself up in it again. There I could see without being seen.

Then I heard a step down the hall. Boot heels clicking. It had to be Pa!

5. "To Lazy Heart Ranch"

IN SUDDEN WILD energy I brushed a nurse out of my way and fled to his arms. "Papa!" I cried. "Oh, Papa!" Starved for his love, I burrowed my head into his rough jacket. He smelled sweet of hay and horses and leather and apples. He held me tight for a long time, and there we stood in my little cell of a room clinging to each other, rocking back and forth, not saying a word.

Then my loving feelings suddenly snapped. I thought, Let him look at me like I am. Suddenly I wanted to say, *Look! Look what you and Mom did to me!* I wrenched violently away and flaunted my face at him.

A nurse started to come in, but she whirled about like a mustang afraid of being trapped. Papa still did not speak. He put his big hands around my face and cradled it ever so gently as if it were a hurt bird. Then he leaned his head down on my stubbly new-growing hair and wept like a child. I could feel his shoulders heaving and the hot tears dampening my scalp. In quick shame I knew that Pa was the one to be pitied. He and Mom thought they were doing the greatest good in the world for me, but the good had backfired like Grandpa's old flintlock.

We didn't talk much on the long way home over the beautiful Sierras that I loved. So much had changed. We were riding in a painted-over truck instead of a wagon drawn by one of our shiny-rumped teams. Papa explained. "Long and short of it is, Annie, it don't pay to haul by wagon any more."

A terrible thought came to me. The horses—were they

gone? "Papa!" I cried. "You haven't sold Hobo and . . ."

"'Course not, child."

Satisfied, we both lapsed into silence. I felt strangely uplifted. I forgot about my face. My prison term was over and all joy had not been squeezed out of me. I could run. I would ride again. I drank deep of my freedom. The sun swam in a blue bowl of sky that was almost empty of clouds— only scraps of white wool caught on the saw-toothed peaks. I couldn't tell which was snow, which cloud.

April lay on the land. Miles on miles of April—greening over the mountains, fuzzing over the meadows, and the air so clean and fine I gulped it in great lungfuls. A doe deer and a buck bounded across the road in front of us. I laughed, watching until their white tails flashed out of sight.

It was plain as anything that God still cared for me. Why else had He left me all His creation? More contented than I had been in months, I fell into a deep sleep, my head in Papa's lap. Not until we were alongside the Truckee River, winding down through the meadows on its banks did I waken.

Papa picked up our talk where we'd left off. "We're going to need 'em more than ever now."

"The horses?"

"Yep. And I'll be needing a good young hand around the new place. One who can drive and ride and muck out and mend harness and paint and shingle . . ."

The new place? What did Pa mean?

"That is," he added without ever meeting my gaze, "if your back's done hurtin', and your neck."

"Oh, yes!" I answered quickly. "Even over the bumps I scarce noticed a thing."

"Good!" he said with a deep intake of breath. "The new place is down the canyon a piece, just a skip and a holler from Reno. Remember that old road to the Indian reservation?"

"Sure I do. Every time I wore my beaded moccasins at the hospital I closed my eyes and thought about our visits with the Paiutes and old Chief Many Feathers."

"Reno's just getting too big," Pa said, talking as much to himself as to me. "Sidewalks now 'stead o' good old dirt. A man can't even raise a dust when he walks. And houses pressin' in closer and closer. Why, a feller can hardly breathe."

His hands suddenly tightened on the wheel until the blue

veins flattened to nothing. "Speakin' of houses . . ." the words came slowly now, very slowly ". . . your Mom had to get away from our old house."

I felt a cold clutch of fear. What had happened to my pretty Mom?

"They say . . ." Pa's voice strangled in his throat. He tried again. "They say lightning never hits twice . . ."

"Was our house struck by lightning?"

He gave me a quick-flung glance as if trying to remember I was still only twelve. He spoke faster now. "Two months after you went away, your little brother came down with the polio, too. Only he died."

I reached for Pa's hand. An awed silence came between us. When he finally spoke again, it startled me.

"Pardner," he said when he could steady his voice, "we tried the best way we knew to take care of you. Can't say we did a good job of it, but we tried. Now *you* got to help us."

I squeezed his hand harder.

We kept going, past the old familiar landmarks, past our old home and the barns, and kept right on, still traveling alongside the Truckee but leaving houses behind. City streets gave way to green meadows, and brown cows dotting the landscape like freckles sprinkled lightly. And I loved the vast loneliness and the rimming crags of mountains.

Already I was arranging with my mind to accept the shape in which I'd been re-created. With Mom and Pa needing my help, I would have to figure out a way. Besides, my back didn't hurt any more and I could turn my neck some, and I could see and smell beauty. "Dear God!" I whispered in a sort of prayer. "Your world is beautiful."

We began bearing right, still meandering along the river, and now we turned off the highway, and the truck rattled down a rocky road past a new, unweathered marker. "To Lazy Heart Ranch," it said. And after one more bend we jolted to a stop in front of a long shed, freshly painted white. There was no house anywhere. Only this long shed with an open shelter in the middle and an enclosed place at each end.

Mom came running out of the nearest door. She still looked young and pretty, only thinner. Her eyes were so full of happy tears that she couldn't see me real plain, and while she was hugging me as if she'd never let me go again, I looked over her shoulder and caught movement in the shed at the far end. Above the half-door I saw a pair of ears pricked, then a blazed face bobbed up, and there, miracle of miracles, was my dream—the white barn, the half-door, and *my* horse looking for me.

Arm in arm the three of us, me half-running, pulling Pa and Mom, reached the shed.

"Are you really Hobo?" I whispered. "Why, your coat's slick as a chestnut!"

"And why not!" Pa announced with a proud grin. "Just because he's got a lot o' mature mustang sense, you don't recognize him. And besides, I been grooming him within an inch of his life."

And then Hobo put in his word. He began whinnerin' in that sweet snorty way of his and pawing at the door, and I

didn't care if it was his barley he wanted, or if he was hankerin'
to be out with the other horses, or whether it was me he recognized. I just opened the fancy latch, the likes of which we'd

never had back in Reno, and I went in. And I kissed the blaze on his face like some silly girl who'd never been around horses, and cried all over his shiny neck and his mane, and I didn't care.

After a minute Pa tapped me on the shoulder and pointed to a sheet of paper tacked on the wall. "Stop your muggin' and come see this," he coaxed.

I tore myself away from Hobo and studied Papa's printing. It was a proper-looking bill of sale saying a lot of things I knew already—that Hobo was out of a mustang mare by a mustang sire, and he was a bright buckskin with black points and a blazed face. It also said: *In return for a year's work help-ing to build us a house, I hereby transfer ownership of one Hobo with the Lazy Heart brand to Annie Bronn to have, hold, exercise, and en-joy.* And there was Pa's signature, *Joseph Bronn*, bold and black. And beneath it a dotted line where I was supposed to sign. Dangling from a piggin' string was a new-sharpened pencil.

Joyously I picked it up and wrote with the biggest flourish I knew how,

Annie Bronn

Now Hobo was really, truly mine.

6. *It Takes a Smart Mustang—*

QUICK AS a flash flood, my months of loneliness
washed away. I was my Pa's Pardner again. And
Hobo was my very own, and Foxy and Old Baldy
and Dolly were good as mine, and the mountains and sky
were mine, and the green grass rumpling in the wind, and the
meadow larks trilling like all Heaven was in their throats. Even
the scaredy rabbits and the noisy magpies were my friends. At
last I was free as they were. No casts to imprison me. No cold
white walls to fence me in.

After the ether and Lysol smelliness of the hospital, our
living quarters in the barn were sweet with the scent of horses
and hay. The dirt floor was friendly to bare feet. And the bunk-
beds, sawhorse tables, and orange-crate shelves seemed beautiful as store-bought mahogany. Mom made two rooms out of

one by hanging an Indian blanket over a clothesline. To me it hung prettier than velvet or satin.

Mom never once mentioned my looks, but I caught her putting away her pretty gold-framed mirror that she had saved from her girlhood days. I never let on that I knew why—even when I watched her combing her long hair by guess. My hair was so short I could comb it with my fingers and spit. Of course, if Mom caught me, I had to begin all over with a comb, not the old toothless one that hung on the side of the barn at home, but a brand new one. It had sharp teeth and I hated it.

Mom did everything with a song—even her cooking on an old two-burner plate that took up half the kitchen table. She boiled, stewed, and fried on one burner, and in a tin oven atop the other she baked flaky biscuits and crisp apple fancies that all but melted in your mouth before you could swallow 'em. For the first time in all my life I couldn't get enough to eat, and I'd clean my plate so's Mom never had to scrape it. With honey from our own bees and eggs from our own hens, breakfast was worth getting up for.

Bathing was a hit-or-miss affair in a galvanized tub behind the Indian blanket. As I soaped and splattered and rinsed, I felt gawky as a stork in a canary dish.

Except for eating, sleeping, and bathing, I spent no time at all in the house. It seemed as if Nature grabbed me by the hand and pulled me outside. I had to bask in, wallow in, work and play in all outdoors.

We had our own small sea of grass along the banks of the Truckee, and that's where I spent my days. It was alive with little creatures—ladybugs and lizards, deer mice and chick-arees, pocket gophers and jackrabbits. Pa always called them "jackass rabbits," but Mom forbade me to say it. Occasionally deer came down out of the hills and scrubbed their tongues at our salt licks, and once a spotted owl perched on my head, quiet as a sigh.

Much as I'd dreamed of my own horse looking out over the half-door, pining for me, I knew now that was city stuff, for horses who had never run wild. Almost the first thing I did was to give Hobo all the freedom of the Lazy Heart Ranch. Snorting his thanks, he exploded out the door, sunfishing at the sky. Then he lined out for the open meadow. I could picture him leaping the fence, racing on and on until he was clean out of sight. Instead, he rounded up Dolly and Foxy and Old Baldy and told them he was still boss of the band.

It was a long time before he entered his private stall again. Only once did he go there of his own free will. It had been sleeting all night, and in the morning I rushed out to see if he and the others were blanketed with ice. To my surprise, they were steamy warm, all four of them crowded and cozy in Hobo's stall, with the bottom half of the door closed! Pa said that Dolly had surely pushed down the bar, her being so motherly. But of course I knew it was Hobo.

Water for the horses came from the irrigation canal nearby. Once a week Pa would raise a gate to let water gush into the ditches. Then it would be a big flow, enough for the horses to splash knee-deep. But other times it was only a trickle.

My first weeks at home were full of wonder and happiness.

Then, gradually, almost without my knowing, a small worry crept in. Pa stayed home so much, and he even had time to ride with me. How was he earning any money? And what about Mom? She seemed happy enough now with our picnic way of life. But when she grew older, like Grandma, wouldn't she want a real house to live in? Why didn't we begin building it?

I said nothing of my worry, but tried to be Pa's strong right arm and help him more as I grew bigger and stronger. We raised alfalfa hay to sell to cattle ranchers for winter forage, and I drove the mower around the field while Hobo and Dolly nodded their heads as we made smaller and ever smaller circles.

In time Pa let me drive the dump rake, too. He and Charley Johnston, a neighbor boy, heaved the hay on top of the wagon and I was allowed to build the load.

Charley was six years older than I, and distant kin to the Delaware Indians. In some ways he was a lot like them, even though he didn't have their dark eyes or hair. But his skin was browned by desert sun. If he'd been naked with only a breechclout like the Indians used to wear, and if he'd ridden our Old Baldy bareback, they'd have looked all of one piece.

Pa admired Charley and was loud in his praise. "That young feller," he told Mom, "is rugged and steadfast as the mountains, and brave enough to spit in a cougar's eye."

It was Charley who finally helped Mom to get her house. Of course, Pa birthed the idea. Then he and Charley, with all our horses pulling, dragged home three old boxcars discarded by the railroad. By knocking out the ends and snugging them together, they built as cozy a house as any beaver's. What I liked about it was the way it formed a kind of U with a long room on each side. This left garden space open to the sky, where we could plant a willow tree and picnic in its shade. In spite of Mom's fears I helped with the shingling, just like I'd promised. It was scary up on that high slidy roof, but I wouldn't let on, especially to Charley.

We kept working on the house after school began that fall. Sometimes Charley and I rode out on the wide sage-stubbled ranges to find old wagon wheels to make a gate and to outline Mom's flower bed. I was glad he liked to ride, because Mom wouldn't let me ride alone. During school hours I studied like mad just to be free in the evening for Hobo and the rest of the horses. Was it a guilty feeling I had? Was I trying to make up to them for Pa's taking 'em away from their mountains? If truth were known, I thought far more of them than of my schoolmates; they ranked right alongside Mom and Pa.

As for my feelings for Charley, I kind of lumped him with all outdoors. I never thought about him much until several years went by. By then I had a high school diploma with honors in shorthand and typing. The first time I began thinking about Charley as a person was on the Saturday he came over to borrow Hobo.

"Quick, Annie!" he said. "It's an emergency!"

"What is?"

"The Grafs' new Appaloosey got away and he's headin' clean for Idaho 'cause he just came from there."

I knew the Grafs prized their spotted stallion, whom they'd named Chief-Thunder-Rolling-in-the-Mountains and Chief Thunder for short. They planned to use him to breed up their cow ponies. "But why Hobo?" I asked.

"Because it takes a smart mustang to catch a smart one."

"You may take Hobo," I said grandly, "if I can go along."

Charley didn't hide his irritation. " 'Course you can go. But you're not the best roper in Nevada, you know."

All the while we were arguing, Charley was straightening the saddle blanket, setting the saddle, tightening the cinch on Hobo, and I was doing the same to Foxy.

We paced out slowly until we were dead certain of Chief Thunder's trail. First readings were plain. He was heading for Idaho all right, and by the way his hindfeet were over-stepping his front ones he must have been traveling fast as an antelope. Our horses broke into a long smooth lope.

We passed the Painted Rocks where the river breaks out of the Truckee Canyon, then skirted the Indian huts at Wadsworth, and lined out across the sandy flats toward the Nightingale Range. I was content to bring up the rear, letting Charley and Hobo do the tracking. I meant to keep my mind on the runaway but I began day-dreaming about the Paiutes who had once lived here in peace. And in my dreaming I was on their side, an Indian girl, raging in fury at the white men who chopped down our piñon trees for firewood. How could we survive the winter without meaty pine nuts to grind into flour? And how could we hunt deer when the white man had fenced off the watering places for their stupid cows?

Charley and I were traveling too fast for talk, but not as fast as my thoughts. It was a rough old road Chief Thunder had taken, and we flew in solitude in the sizzling summer sun, stopping only to make sure of the hoofprints.

Whoa! A drift fence ahead with a cattle-guard! Chief Thunder knew what to do. He had detoured, gone down to the river for a splash and a drink, then up and around the end of the drift fence, and on his way. We let our horses do the same.

Revived, we gave chase—across greasewood flats, around buckbrush and sage, over rocks and dry washes. Suddenly Charley pulled up. He signaled off to the right with his chin. And there, on a rise of rock, bold against the sky, stood Chief Thunder. His head and ears were pointed to Finger Wash Draw. Then we saw what he had his eyes on—a peaceful bunch of horses grazing. Even with the distance between them you could see the dotted line of fire running from Chief Thunder to the others. He was totally unaware of us, unaware of anything but the mares in the bunch.

Charley and Hobo sneaked up on him, noiseless as smoke, Charley making his loop. The second that rope went sailing through the air the stallion reared and leaped half way to Heaven, but Charley had counted on that leap and all in an

instant the noose settled over Chief Thunder's shoulders. Hobo slammed on the brakes. The Chief went clean over and hit the earth with a thump. One brief struggle and he gave up. He had been caught before! Meekly he came along with Hobo and Foxy.

I felt almost sorry we had found him. He had looked so free, standing there against the sky. But then I remembered how much the Grafs needed him.

All three horses were winded and leg-weary, so we slow-footed most of the long way home. Now there was time for talk, and Charley told me bits and pieces of his life. It came as a shock to learn that loneliness had been part of his child-hood, too. His long-ago Delaware ancestor had given him blood that was full of restlessness. At sixteen he ran away to Mexico and joined in a drive to wage war on the cattle rustlers. Then alone he pushed northward, living on wild game, killing only what he needed.

The shadows of the mountains lengthened across the flats as Charley talked on, remembering places and people and dangers—the rattlesnake who tangled with him over the same pigeon. "That daggone diamondback slid off a ledge and quick as lightning stabbed me in the shoulder."

"Whatever did you do?"

"I rode fast for help, but everything began blurring, and I fell off my horse and got back on and fell off again. I don't know how I reached that grizzled old wonderful doctor."

I felt a curious fascination for this life that was so different from my own. I was longing to ask him why he had run away from home, but he wouldn't have heard me. His mind had already gone on. He was thinking out loud. The horses and I kept our ears pricked for every word.

"Seems like Nature's been my foster mother," he said. "She taught me the important things, like the sense of wonder when an animal or a bird trusts you. And the friendly quiet of the hills where you can be alone, yet not lonely. And the everlasting joy of freedom."

It was the first time that anyone had ever spoken his heart to me. I had no words to reply. I could only jog on in complete happiness. By the time we reached home Charley had become a person, a friend; he was no longer just a piece of sun and sky.

Right after that I asked Mom to put up her mirror again, and I began experimenting with my hair.

7. Operation Rescue

AFTER CATCHING the runaway, Hobo became a somebody. "Takes a smart mustang to catch a smart one" echoed all up and down the canyon. His reputation spread like rabbit brush. Two weeks later—on a blazing Sunday in August—his fame reached its peak. I was alone in the house. Mom and Pa had gone to a funeral in Reno. I had just wiped and put away the last dish and was pulling on my boots when I heard hoofs pounding hard up our road.

I rushed out, one boot on, and through the cloud of dust made out the figure of Eli Pike, a neighbor. Elbows flapping, he was riding his old mule hell-bent for leather. At the gate he slid to a stop and hollered through the dust: "Annie! Get your Pa! My dang fool cows are caught in the bog below the railroad bridge and ———"

"Pa's gone!" I yelled back.

He didn't hear me. He hollered louder. "Two's already kilt by the Californy express." He was in whispering distance now, but he roared louder than ever. "The rest of 'ems scairt and wallerin' in the bog." And in the same breath, "My missus's going to have a baby, and Doc's gone away. I got to help her."

The old black mule was wheezing and sighing. I took hold of the rope-bridle and rubbed his steaming neck. Then I tried to calm Mr. Pike. "Don't you worry, sir. You go home and help Mrs. Pike. I'll get Hobo; he's the best ropin' horse anywhere around. We'll save your cows."

"Not you!" Eli Pike shouted in disgust. Then he wailed, "I want your Pa!"

Now I lost my temper. "I been telling you! He and Mom are gone!"

At last he heard me. He jerked the mule's head around, jabbed his heels into the bony ribs, and took off. Almost out of earshot he yelled back, "I'm goin' fer Charley."

I thought, There's no time to wait for Charley! He could be any place on Sunday, fly-fishing or hunting, or even prospecting up in the hills. I flew to the barn and pulled the dinner bell. The horses came galloping in, Hobo in the lead. With quick fingers I saddled up, trying not to show my haste. The Pikes needed those cattle! There were six children already,

67

not counting the one unborn. With all of those children, they needed every single cow.

I took Pa's lariat out of the tin where he kept it carefully coiled and threw it over the horn of my saddle. I swung aboard Hobo and headed for the bridge. Pa had taught me how to rope. We'd practiced on Orphie, our stray hound, which I haven't even mentioned until now because just when he got to feel at home with us, he was run over. He was a big gentle fellow, and every time I roped him we gave him a biscuit; so he just let himself be caught.

But this was different! Even if I did rope each cow and Hobo pulled her to safety, what about the trains coming and going? This was the Southern Pacific Railroad and for fifteen miles it ran on a single track. Trains whizzed by as if the faster they flew the less likely they were to crash head on.

Soon I reached the bridge high above the Truckee, and there below, trapped in the backwash of the river, I saw the cows. Hobo and I climbed the slope onto the cindery railbed. We stopped just short of the bridge. It had an open floor with wide-apart ties through which you could see the flow of the river twenty feet below. No horse could walk on it.

I held Hobo short-reined, figuring how to save the terrified creatures without Hobo getting hurt. The risk was not the open bed of the bridge, but the fast express trains. What were the chances of rescuing the cows with Hobo pulling them from a lariat-length away? I looked at my watch. We had barely a half-hour before the next train.

The cattle were struggling below in their slimy mud trap.

They were bawling and scared. One injured heifer lay at the foot of the embankment where a train had flung her. I was plenty scared too, until I heard hoofbeats and turned to see Charley riding up with two of the Pike girls holding on behind. From the way Charley's eyes squinted I knew he was figuring things out. Right away he ground-tied his horse on firm footing beyond the bog. Then he scrambled up the embankment, pulling the girls along like rag dolls. He set them down on the track and barked out his orders.

"Clara! Run down to that bend in the track. Watch for the train coming from the east, but keep in sight of Annie and the bridge. Emma! You run across the bridge to where you can see the train coming from the west."

Both girls started to their posts, but Charley stopped them. "Wait! Listen! Here's what you got to do. The moment you see smoke or hear a train whistle, signal to Annie. Scream like you're being scalped. Pull off your neckerchief. Wave it like crazy in case your voice don't carry."

He turned to me now and barked out more orders: "Annie! Sit tight on Hobo. Take a double dally around that horn. If the train comes, drop the dally, back Hobo like a bat out of hell, whirl him off the track and get down off that embankment, fast!

"Now I'll go down and hook onto one of the critters. With me pushing and Hobo pullin' we'll save all—all but that one on her side. 'Pears to me she's broken her leg." His mouth twisted as if he hated what he had to do.

Then quickly he skidded down the bank toward the cows.

In the way he worked now I began to understand Charley's compassion for every living creature. He was like a vet on a battlefield, separating the hopeless from the strong. I watched him pull his gun, heard the crack of it, saw the suffering heifer go limp. There was a nervous shying of the cows, but Charley's voice calmed them. Then he went to work, looping the rope around the neck of the nearest one. Now his upflung hand said, "Ready!"

Hobo felt my signal. He veered sharply to the left. He braced himself for the pull, then hunkered down, squatting on his haunches, backing, straining, pulling the scrambling cow up and out of the sucking mud. There was no time to look at my watch. I could only pay attention to Hobo, see that he was on solid footing, keep the rope taut until at last the mud-wet creature stood on firm ground.

I heaved a sigh. One was safe. Quickly I rode ahead to slacken the rope so that Charley could remove it to loop the next cow. I watched him rope another, and just as he gave me the signal an ear-splitting scream tore the air. Instantly Charley freed the cow. I remembered my orders. I dropped the dally, backed Hobo along the roadbed, whirled him off the track, and together we plunged down the embankment just before the fast express hitting eighty miles an hour hissed by in a swirl of dust and thunder.

Not until the last car had passed did Hobo and I begin to tremble. I could feel his heartbeats thudding against the calf of

my leg and my own heart pounding fiercely. There was no time to do more than stroke his neck and talk soft. Only forty-five minutes before the east-bound train! But now there was no need to worry about the blind turns; we could depend on our scouts.

Charley, Hobo, and I worked like a team. Push, pull; struggle and sweat. Let the sweat run down your face, under your arms, down your back. No time to wipe it. No time to wipe the lather on Hobo's neck. No time for anything but pull and push, and listen for screams and train whistles, and back and maneuver, and watch the train fly by with the staring faces in the windows and the waving hands. And we too weak to wave. Just the job ahead. And one by one the huddle of cows growing on firm ground.

At last high noon overhead and the job done. And ten creatures safe. And Hobo a hero. And Charley my idol.

8. Our Small Happy World

THAT NIGHT I solemnly resolved I would someday marry Charley Johnston. Mom seemed to applaud my decision without a word spoken between us. First thing she did was to buy me my own mirror. It was one of those stand-up affairs with roses and daisies growing all over its frame, and right away I felt prettier. Mom and I practiced in front of it, first on my hair. Luckily I had a good healthy crop of hair, long and thick as a stallion's mane. But, ugh, the color! In a horse we'd call it mouse-brown, and that's just what it was. Mom and I overlooked the color. Night after night we took turns brushing—hard and fierce. Then Mom plaited it in tight little braids, and that's how I slept. Mornings we shook it out and admired how it rippled and shone, like the tail of a pampered show horse.

Then we practiced piling it higher on one side of my head to give an optical illusion to my out-of-line features. *Optical illusion!* This was a term I'd learned in school, meaning something that looks like something it is not. But now it meant something wonderful and special, like a life belt thrown out to save me from drowning in loneliness.

On Grandma's old sewing machine Mom made me some riding shirts of softest cambric in bright flower colors—buttercup yellow and nasturtium reds and orange. "These shades make your hair positively russet!" Mom said approvingly.

Papa, bless his heart, noticed the difference. At supper one night he looked at me over his coffee cup, his deepset eyes smiling. "It's like magic," he said, turning to Mom. "Our ugly duckling has flown the coop. You've hatched out a swan."

I ran around the table and hugged him hard. His praise was all I needed to spur me on.

Next I practiced walking, holding my low shoulder as high as I could without wincing, and my high shoulder low. All at once it came to me that if I didn't stand face-to-face with a person but slightly at an angle, how could he tell that I wasn't built straight as the Ponderosa pines?

It worked! The mirror was better than any charm school. Each time I smiled into it, I seemed transformed. All the years of pain washed away. I couldn't get over the miracle. Finally Mom had to trim my sails. She caught me spending too much time grinning at myself, laughing into the mirror, experimenting. Her voice was soft as a caress but the words had a bite. "Smiles are good as a tonic for giver and receiver alike," she said, "that is, if given sincere. But take care you don't become a Cheshire cat. The smile's got to be from a deep-in, loving gladness."

Poor unsuspecting Charley! He never knew I was changing because of him. I wasn't sure he even noticed until one day we were out riding, hunting Indian relics. Suddenly he reached over, snatched off my wide-brimmed cowboy hat and plopped it atop his own. "Annie," he said gravely, "anyone with hair like brown sunshine oughtn't ever to wear a hat."

It was enough happiness to last for a long time, and it had to. Months went by before Charley seemed to notice me again. Perhaps it was because we were all faced with the

terror of change. Pa had been offered a job by the Dodge Transfer people back in Reno, and Mom just had to agree because the ranch wasn't paying.

It was on my eighteenth birthday that Charley came over for a kind of farewell supper. Mom had baked a cake with enough winking candles to make up for the sadness we were feeling. After supper, with dishes put away, Charley sort of steered me out onto the porch. It put me in mind of the way one horse will drive another to a certain spot. The moonlight was bright out there and it spilled down through our willow tree like a waterfall.

"Annie," he said with a touch of lostness as if already we'd moved away, "you're so beautiful. In all ways." There were great pauses between his words. "Outward, and on the inside, too." Still he did not take my hand.

"I?" My voice was a whisper of wonder. I wanted to say, "Beauty is in the eye of the beholder," but I couldn't say anything. There was a crumb of cake on his cheek that needed brushing, and my hand went out of itself and brushed the crumb away.

"Marry me, Annie," he said, not putting a question mark after the words. His eyes were troubled as if all the lonely years were piling up behind them and might explode if I didn't say yes.

He searched my face and saw the answer, and knew too that I couldn't talk for crying.

Charley bought the Lazy Heart Ranch from Pa, bought the horses and all. That is, he made a down payment. And he applied to the registrar of brands to change the name so he'd feel a part of it. He added another heart to the brand and called it the *Double* Lazy Heart.

Charley knew we had an uphill climb to make the ranch pay, but he didn't dream how steep that hill would be. Late at night I'd wake up and find him at the kitchen table, chewing on a stub of a pencil, adding up columns of figures on the backs of our bills. Always he got the same chilling answer. "No matter how I reckon it, Annie—even if we get three crops a year—it won't bring in enough."

Maybe it was Charley, or maybe it was me, or maybe it was one of those breathless moments when two people in love pounce on the same idea at the same time. Anyway, we figured there were a lot of lonely children in Reno, city children who had never been on a horse, who had never been friendly with earth and sky and birds and deer and lizards and rabbits.

"Let's have a weekend dude ranch for children!" one or the other of us shouted. "We can sleep them all over the place."

" 'Course we can."

Charley said, "The barn loft is a fine place to bed down."

"Ummm! Smells nice. They'd love it."

"And I could put up pup tents out in the fields for the adventure-loving boys."

"And I could sew up some mummy bags for timid girls who want to sleep in the house . . . even on the floor."

"And with my harmonica we could have sings around a fire, and we could fish in the Truckee, and ride the range, and prospect for gold."

In no time at all the Double Lazy Heart opened its gates to a bunch of wild buckaroos whose shouts and laughter bounced across the canyon from mountain to mountain.

Charley and I adored our hilarious weekends with house and barn full of children. Once when a tousled redhead asked, "How do you park a horse when you want to stop?" we laughingly decided to do a book and call it "Our Weekend Children." But we never wrote the book; we were too busy living it.

Besides, I had to take a secretarial job in Reno to make ends meet. This was no hardship, for I liked to pound out words on a typewriter, even if they weren't my own. And I felt a sense of excitement in being part of a busy office; it was like playing in a big orchestra with other people clicking away on their keyboards, phones ringing, papers rattling, deep voices booming, sopranos answering.

My days now were full to bursting. Twenty-six miles to work each morning. Twenty-six miles back at night. Mountains of groceries to buy for the weekends. Games to plan. Treasure hunts on horseback. Gymkhanas. Lessons to prepare on flora and fauna. Specimens to collect.

I had few adult friends these days, and these few felt sorry for me. But I couldn't have been happier. For what could have been more thrilling than watching a frightened caterpillar of a child grow butterfly wings? I'll always remember one, an overfat lump of a boy who had to be lifted up on a horse and led about time after time. I baked him a three-layered chocolate cake with whipped cream frosting to celebrate the day when at last he swung into the saddle by himself and trotted off in time to his own self-confident whistling!

And there was awkward Emmy Luke, with skinny arms and legs too long for the rest of her. She took to running away and hiding behind the pump house. I'd find her there, all tear-sodden because the other children made fun of her. It was Hobo who gave her a sense of belonging. First he walked with her as carefully as if the slightest jarring might break her thin little body. Then he put on the gentlest dogtrot that made Charley smile swiftly, secretly at me. Hobo seemed to be in on our conspiracy.

But the thing that gave Emmy Luke real importance happened on the day we were riding three abreast across an open plank bridge over a gulley. I was on the outside riding Pepper Pot, a rough-broke cayuse we'd had to take in trade for a ton of hay. In the middle rode a brand-new girl on Foxy, and Hobo with Emmy Luke was on the far side. Of course, I knew better than to ride three abreast in a spot like this, but everything had been smooth as honey till now. Suddenly out of nowhere a bird flew screaming in Pepper Pot's face. He shied and bumped into Foxy, who in turn shied against Hobo. For one panicky moment I could see Emmy Luke tossed off into the rocks below. Instead, Hobo braced himself against Foxy, and held all of us on the bridge.

At lunchtime the new girl said, "Guess what, kids."

Forks and spoons paused.

"What?" somebody asked, his mouth full of potato.

"Emmy Luke saved Annie and me from a terrible fall this morning."

After lunch Emmy grabbed me around the knees and said with fierce intensity, "Oh, Annie, I love Hobo so." Then she turned her rainbow face to me. "I love you too, Annie."

"And I love *you*," I said, squeezing her hard. For I did. I loved her and the big sky and the wide earth and the bare brown mountains and all its creatures.

Who knows if I might have become bored with happiness, like too much ice cream or too much anything? Our worries all seemed to be melting away. We were getting three crops of hay and selling it as fast as Charley could harvest it; the list of dudes wanting to come to the ranch was long as a kite's tail; we were a month ahead on our mortgage payments. And wonder of earth and of Heaven, Charley still thought me beautiful. Some people have the Midas touch, but Charley made everything he touched seem beautiful.

One fall evening when we had cooked our supper outdoors and we both felt drenched in happiness, I said a poem to Charley. He wasn't one for poetry; he enjoyed harmonica music more. But he liked this one:

> *Prairie goes to the mountain,*
>   *Mountain goes to the sky.*
> *The sky sweeps across to the distant hills*
> *And here, in the middle,*
>   *Am I.*
>
> *Shadows creep up the mountain,*
>   *Mountain goes black on the sky,*
> *The sky bursts out with a million stars*
> *And here, by the campfire,*
>   *Am I.*

"*Am I* means *Are we*, doesn't it, Annie?"

"Of course it does."

"Heaven is on earth for us."

"*Now* it is," I said, "but it wasn't always, for me."

"Nor me."

We sat there in the living sleeping silence of night, my hand lost in Charley's and one of the stray pups curled close by us for warmth. We were caught up in the silver web of the moon, caught up in our small happy world.

I thought, There's nothing more in life that I want.

9. More Dead than Alive

NEXT MORNING I was still in a state of bliss. Our day began early, as always. Charley was planning to bale the dried alfalfa and I was off to Reno to be a prim and proper secretary. Humming an old cowboy song, I kissed him good-bye, laughing at his parting words, "Only birds can sing and peck at the same time. Good-bye, my bluebird!"

I liked driving to the city in the early morning. And this morning especially. The sun was edging up around the mountains, and high on Mount Rose two dollops of snow were dark-wetting the slope as they melted and came trickling down to join the Truckee River.

Like any dyed-in-the-wool rancher I smiled at the precious moisture. "The Truckee needs all she can get," I thought.

I sniffed the air. It was still cool and sweet. My sandwich and an apple lay on the seat beside me, and the camera with its expensive color film that we saved only for miracles, like the double rainbow I'd once caught. Beside it lay a book to read at lunchtime. I can still remember its title: *The Sea of Grass*. I'd chosen it because I hoped it would tell of long-ago days when the old West was an ocean of grass that billowed on and on until the mountains put an end to it; and herds of buffalo and wild horses roamed free, and were free for the taking.

It was still too early for traffic. My little roadster hummed along at full speed. I'd get to the office ahead of time, and Mr. Harris, my boss, would nod in pleasure. Then we'd whiff through the morning's mail, and soon it would be noon and for a whole wonderful hour I could lose myself in the wind-rumpled miles of grass.

Suddenly I stopped day-dreaming. An enormous cattle truck loomed in front of me. I drove up close, expecting to see white-faced Herefords or shiny black Angus' or gray clouds of sheep.

Then my hands clutched the wheel and my throat knotted at what I saw. The truck was jammed, crammed, packed with mustangs, more dead than alive! Tatters of flesh hung loose on their necks. Blood trickled from their nostrils. They had the look and stench of death. All that kept them on their feet was the way they were wedged in.

The shock stunned me. My ears rang; the earth whirled. Dizzily, I stumbled out of the car and vomited by the side of the road. When the earth steadied again I got back in and raced desperately after the truck. For miles I trailed the monster as it roared along the pavement, belching black fumes in my face. Sick at heart I speeded up, then slowed, keeping the truck just in sight, trying not to look at any one animal. I felt as though I were part of something terrible, horrible, unclean. Where were the mustangs being taken? Why were they in such condition? I had to know.

At a stop sign I came up close and a little foal with a blaze just like Hobo's tried to poke his head through the bars. He was staring out at me in wild appeal, as if somehow it was my fault, and why didn't I lift a finger to help? I could feel the solid boards of the truck crushing against his chest, against my chest too. They were like prison bars! Suddenly I was back in the hospital, my lungs bursting for breath, my fingernails clawing at the cast.

Questions flooded my brain. Who was responsible? What could I do? Pa's words rang in my ears: "Torture is the unforgivable sin." Unafraid now, I kept on following, even as the truck pulled off the highway onto a narrow dirt road. The landscape grew lonely and desolate, with no cabins or ranches. Just bare gray earth, and bare brown mountains, and tumbleweeds dead and forlorn.

I looked at my gauge; the tank was half full. I looked at my watch. The office would be at its busiest now. Everyone would be wondering about me. As I followed the truck on and on, the gentle morning sunshine gave way to merciless heat. Blood and sweat crusted on the horses' bodies. Heads bobbed nervously, then drooped low, and lower. I could see their muscle tremors and their breath coming fast, as if they

were being pursued. The dizziness came on me again. Frantically I clung to the wheel and began saying a prayer I'd found in the hospital library. I didn't know I'd memorized it, but now I chanted it over and over—to steady my hands on the wheel, to stop the reeling earth, to stop the squeezing of my stomach.

"See, Lord,[*]
my coat hangs in tatters;
all that I had of zest,
all my strength,
I have given.
Now my poor head swings
to offer up all the loneliness of my heart.
Dear God,
stiff on my thickened legs
I stand here before You,
Your useless servant.
Oh! Of Your goodness,
give me a gentle death."

And I prayed for the death of those horses.

The truck was turning into a narrow, dusty byway. I cranked my windows tight; still the dust seeped in. The horses were all but lost in it.

At last the truck came to a stop in front of a low brick building. Above the door, in ragged crimson letters, as if painted in blood, were the words: Rendering Plant.

I slowed to a stop. In my daze I wanted *not* to look, but I was hypnotized. Two brawny men were lowering the tailgate of the truck. To my horror I saw that some of the horses were hobbled, hindfoot to forefoot! Now their feet were jerked

* "The Prayer of the Old Horse," from *Prayers from the Ark*, by Carmen Bernos de Gasztold.

out from under them, and on their sides they were pulled like cold carcasses across the tailgate and into the plant. Only their heaving bodies showed they were still breathing.

I knew now why they had not been killed. They had to be brought in alive or their flesh would have rotted in the sun. But at last death would come. It might not be gentle, but surely it would be swift. And then their meat would be ground and stuffed into cans.

In fierce rage I flipped open my camera and snapped pictures of the grim scene. One of the men saw me and stalked over to my car. He thrust his dark-bearded face close to mine.

"Listen, you dumb sob-sister," he snarled, "you burn them pictures, or I'll——"

I whirled the car about, and he half fell out of my way, firing a volley of curses after me.

Somehow I arrived at the office. Oh, the peace of it! The low-toned voices. The whisper of papers. The whir of type-writers. Eyes followed me asking, Why are you late? But I explained only to Mr. Harris.

"I can understand your feelings, Annie," he said. "You were thinking of your own Hobo and what he's meant to you."

"Not only of him. But because of him I feel kin to his whole tribe. That's why I've got to do something to stop this cruelty. Something! Anything!"

Mr. Harris shook his head in concern. "Annie," he said, "the demand for horsemeat to feed dogs and cats and even chickens has become big business. So big now that the hunters can afford to ride roundup in their own private planes. They're not just Nevadans, either. They come from other states."

I was shocked. "Do you mean that the little planes I often see skimming low over the foothills could be mustangers?"

"That's exactly what I mean. And those pilots are a tough bunch; they want no slip of a girl messing in their business. You'd better leave them alone."

"Oh, I'll get men to fight them. Not me," I promised.

Charley had been baling all day and looked sunbeat and tired when I reached home. I waited until after supper to tell him. When I explained all I had seen and learned about the mustangers, he put down his cup of coffee and his face had a look of deep pain and sadness.

He stared out at the far mountains, his eyes seeming to see everything—not just the truck jam-packed with the mustangs, but the plane roaring out of the sky, flushing them from the foothills, hazing them onto the dry lake beds, then the trucks taking over, chasing them, running them, and running and running them until they dropped. He caught his breath as if he had been running alongside the terrified horses. Angrily he shoved his chair back. He went over to his rifle on the wall and stood there, playing his fingers along the barrel.

When at last he could speak, his voice came deadly slow. "As a boy, my hero was a hard-ridin' cowboy name of Charles Russell, and he used to say: 'The tops of the mountains belong to God and He don't want his wild things disturbed.' That's my creed too."

"Oh, Charley!" I gulped in relief. "I knew you'd help."

"Count on it!" he said, his hands clenched into fists. "We've been so blinded by happiness we let these roundups go on right under our noses. Now, Annie, we got a mighty rough road ahead of us."

"I know. But if we don't do something soon, there won't be any mustangs left."

10. Mice and Mustangs

PA FOUND out from Charley that I was in dead earnest about saving the mustangs. He stopped at the office one noon, with a look of pride on his face. "Let's tie on the feed bag, Annie," he said. "Your Pa's got things deep in his mind."

Pa's idea of the feed bag was a brown paper sack filled with cheese-and-peanut-butter crackers and fig newtons from the corner drug store. Today he splurged with brimming cartons of malted milk.

As we ate, we stood in the bright sunshine on the bridge just outside the office. Munching away, we looked down at the Truckee River bubbling under the bridge and between the tall buildings. Pa's eyes were fixed on a big-chested duck riding the waves like an ocean-going liner. When the duck flew away in answer to a honk in the sky he turned to me. "Annie," he said, "bein' as you're a girl, you got to be extry careful."

I squirmed, thinking he was going to lecture me about my being too skinny and puny to put up a fight. "Careful of what?" I burst out. *"Of what?"*

"Of bein' girrrlish." And he rolled the rr's in disdain. "You can't just rage and gnash your teeth and cry about wild mustangs kicking up dust in the moonlight. That's 'zackly what the flyin' mustangers and the cowmen and sheepmen and all the legal folk are goin' to expect from a girrrl. What I mean is, you got to shock 'em with facts hard as bullets. Annie," he shook his head, "you got a terrible rough road to travel."

I grinned. "You've been talking to a certain Charley Johnston."

"That I have. And I don't aim to interfere with the way you two go about this," he said, waving his fig newton. "That is, after today. Today all I got to say is: Look like a girl. Be a girl. But think reasonable like your Pa." And the smile in his eyes spread across his face until it showed the dark hole where two back teeth were missing. Suddenly he turned off the smile the way you'd switch off a lamp. "Remember, Pardner," he said with gruff tenderness, "don't fire your gun unless its loaded."

Right there, with the noon office people and shoppers passing by, I threw my arms around Pa. "Don't you worry," I cried eagerly, "if facts are what they want, I'll furnish 'em."

With Pa's words ringing in my ears, I set out at once to plan my campaign. To begin with, I went to the local newspapers, urging them to report the cruelties of the plane and truck roundups. The first skirmish came almost before I was ready. It began with a whispered telephone conversation at midnight.

A woman's hushed voice said, "This is Lura Tularski."

I recognized the name at once. I read her "Saddle Chatter" column in the *Journal* the way Mom reads her Bible. Lura discussed the horse world—important things, like the difference between a Thoroughbred and a purebred; and that Arabians have one less vertebra than other horses, which accounts for their short backs; and the special jargon of horse markings, such as stars and stripes, and stockings and socks.

Now in a cloak-and-dagger voice she spoke rapidly. "Listen sharp, Annie. Word has leaked out that the local land management office has given permission to a couple of cowboy pilots from Idaho to round up mustangs in the foothills near your ranch. Maybe you can stop them—if you act quickly."

"Yes, yes!" I whispered in mounting excitement. "But how?"

"Why, just block their permit when they apply to the County Board."

"Wh— when is that?"

"Tomorrow night at eight. They're trying to keep the

meeting secret so there'll be no one on hand to oppose the permit."

"Where's the meeting?"

"In the courthouse at Virginia City. You and Charley have a lot of friends in Storey County, Annie. Round them all up and crash the meeting."

I thanked her and hung up. Aha! I thought. So that's how it's done! Quickly I made my list of names.

At the office next morning I worked fiercely, doing a day's work in four hours. "Mr. Harris," I said at noon, "may I leave now? I've got to help stop a wild horse roundup." Already a plan was forming in my mind.

"How can I say no," Mr. Harris answered, "when your work is already done? But I wish you'd leave mustang business to Charley and the other men."

"Oh, I will," I said honestly enough. "I'll just work in the background. Charley is already calling up everyone he knows will be against it—Tex Gladding, the postmaster at Virginia City; Jack Murry, the guard at the state prison; Attorney Richards and Mr. Flick and all the ranchers in the Truckee meadows."

Before driving home I paid a call at the office of the Bureau of Land Management. I wanted to see for myself what their attitude was. The Supervisor, a pleasant little man with a birdlike fuzz on the top of his head, bowed as politely as if I'd come to tea.

"Hm-m-m," he smiled when I told him my name. "You have a ranch in Storey County, do you not?"

"Yes," I said politely.

Offering me a chair, he began to open up like an oyster to the sun. "I understand there are three hundred pesky mustangs just south of your ranch destroying the grazing land. Is that why you've come to see me?"

"Yes, in a way."

"Well, we plan to do something about it."

"Are there really three hundred?" I asked, trying not to show my doubt.

He nodded, and the fuzz on his head blew ever so slightly. "That's what we figure," he replied. "Our fliers spot a straggle of horses and we know full well that a herd is close by. It's like mice," he added, waggling his forefinger. "Where there's one there's bound to be more."

"Oh?" I said, acting spellbound. And then I noticed a package on his desk labeled Roquefort Cheese, and I figured he'd had more experience with mice than mustangs. Even as he spoke, a tiny dull gray mouse ran up the wall and onto his

desk, sniffing his way to the cheese. There he stood, up on his hind feet, wriggling his whiskers.

I never changed expression.

"Yes, indeed," the man went on, completely unaware of his furry visitor. "But as I say, we plan to do something about it. We do have the power, you know, to order the complete destruction of all wild horses to save what little grass there is. And," he added in obvious pride, "with these air round-ups we can keep the ranges clear for the horses and cattle of ranchers like you, without . . ." here he puffed himself up like a courting pigeon ". . . without costing the taxpayer a cent!"

"How's that, sir?" And I leaned forward so suddenly that the mouse ran down the wall and was gone.

"Why, the rendering plants buy up the horses. At six cents a pound, the fliers are well paid when they round up a whole herd. Yes, ma'am! The Bureau has a fine record for saving the taxpayers' money."

I listened in astonishment.

"At the least, seventy-five thousand mustangs have been captured since I've been here. But our work is far from done. Our manager reports hundreds of wild horses still left in the Virginia ranges."

I thought to myself, How can this be? I have seen only one herd running free in all my lifetime. But I didn't challenge him.

After a polite pause I asked, "When, sir, is the next roundup? And are people permitted to watch?"

"Well . . . ll," he harrumphed, "there are certain matters to be considered as to time and place." The eyes behind their dark-rimmed glasses studied me a moment before continuing. "The pilots must first get a permit from the County Board. Then, of course, it depends on the weather."

"I see."

"The next roundup will be in the range between Lousetown and Ramsey, but a delicate girl like you wouldn't want to watch. No, ma'am! It's not like a rodeo, you know."

Not like a rodeo! No, I could imagine what it would be like. I stood up to leave; I had all the horrible information I needed.

The trim little man stood up, too. "Don't you worry about your own horses, young lady," he smiled reassuringly. "The Bureau does not allow the shooting of any wild horses for fear that branded ones might be killed."

I thought, Is that the only reason?

Feeling dreadfully sick, I hurried home.

11. The Scales Tip Even

THE WONDERFUL thing about Charley was that he was never neutral. As we drove to Virginia City that early June evening, he gripped the wheel hard and I could see his lips moving. He was already blasting off at the meeting.

In the distance, white plumes of steam from Steamboat Springs were puffing out of the ground like train smoke snaking along the horizon.

"I've a head of steam on me, too," Charley said. "I can't wait to blow my top."

I sat closer. In tune.

Virginia City always excited me, mountain-high and mountain-walled as it was. Going there was like reaching for the top of the world. But that night as we wound up and up the steep Geiger Grade, it was like reaching toward something dark and dangerous, and important.

When at last we stopped climbing, the ghost city spread out before us like a picture map. The dying sun had colored it pink and purple and burnt orange, and faint lights were blinking in the houses that clung to the mountainside.

A string of cars was hurrying with us up B Street, past Piper's Opera House. The building was only a husk now, its shingles flapping in the breeze. Just beyond, in solid contrast, the Storey County Courthouse stood, in lawful dignity.

We parked close by and began stomping along the old board walk, our high-heeled boots noisy as horse hoofs. Even the sound of our boots spoke of the urgent purpose and business ahead.

I glanced up at the statue of Justice over the courthouse door. "Look, Charley! She isn't blindfolded like other statues, and her scales tip even." I made him look up. "It's a good omen," I whispered.

Charley wasn't so sure.

Inside, the scene was like a courtroom in an old melodrama, brass spittoons and all. The only difference was the elegant marble fireplace, marble brought over from Italy in the days when the Comstock lode was rich in silver. Now it was a catchall for waste paper and chewed-down cigars.

The county commissioners and the district attorney were already taking their places behind the rail as we walked in. And at a little table by himself, up in the front of the room, sat Lucius Beebe, editor of the famous *Territorial Enterprise*.

I looked around and saw that the audience was split right down the middle, the "fors" on one side, the "agins" on the other. We took seats in the back row among our friends.

"Gads!" the man next to me said. "Looks like we got a hundred head here, all chomping at the bit."

The wall clock pointed precisely to the hour of eight as the chairman rose to his feet. "I'm Bill Marks," he introduced himself, "owner and operator of the Crystal Bar here in Virginia City."

Some in the audience guffawed as if the explanation were unnecessary. They knew him well, even in his off-work clothes.

The man had a scrubbed pink face and a schoolboy grin which vanished the moment he began reading aloud the application for a permit. "To round up by plane," it said, "all unbranded wild horses found on the land between Lousetown and Ramsey."

He leaned over the table now, and spoke directly to two men in the front row. They were dressed differently from us ranchers. They wore shiny black jackets and one wore goggles perched on the back of his head.

"Are you the pilots from Idaho?" Mr. Marks asked.

Like twin mechanical toys, the two fliers hunched forward as one, nodded as one.

Lucius Beebe scratched a few notes on the back of an envelope. The scratching gave me the shivers.

The chairman proceeded. "The names of Gomez and Burger are also on this application. Would one of these gentlemen explain the need for this roundup?"

A chunky, dark-jowled man arose. "I'm Gomez. Own a thousand sheep. And them sneakin' mustangs," he whined, "is over-runnin' my range lands. If somethin' ain't done soon, my sheep'll starve."

Charley and I looked at each other. We had never seen a wild mustang anywhere near our place. I wanted to cry out, "You lie!" But someone did it for me.

"He's a liar!" a weather-beat rancher shouted. "My land abuts his and I ain't seen a band o' wild ones in five year."

Gomez exploded. "I'm tellin' you . . . them scroungy broomtails is eatin' all my forage and spoilin' my land."

An old man on our side of the aisle struggled to his feet, knee joints cracking. "Mr. Chair," he said in his high old-man's voice, "that feller is yawpin' about land that ain't even his'n. He leases it from the Bee-yuoro of Land Management." He stumbled over the word "Bureau", and the "fors" laughed the old man down.

Bill Marks rapped for quiet. "The gentleman is right. We all know that everybody leases his land. Let's hear from the Bureau man."

My acquaintance of the afternoon eagerly jumped to his feet. A wall light made a halo of the duck fuzz on his head as he waited for the question.

"How many wild horses," the chairman asked, "do'you reckon there are here in Storey County?"

"At least three hundred," was the quick reply. Then gulping a breath, the little man began spitting out statistics: "Eighty per cent of Nevada is federal land, and I don't need to tell you ranchers that it takes sixty acres to feed a cow and her calf, and almost as much to feed a ewe and her lamb."

Lucius Beebe belched, as if the remark made him slightly ill.

The man went on, ignoring the interruption. "My Bureau is responsible for keeping the number of wild animals reduced for the benefit of the men who raise cattle and sheep. And we are proud . . . Yes sir! We are proud . . ." here he beamed on his audience, both sides of the aisle ". . . that in conducting these roundups the only expense to the taxpayer is the building of temporary corrals for holding the horses."

Before he could sit down, Jack Murry, the prison guard from Carson City, was on his feet. He turned directly to the Bureau man. "But in this case," he said, quietly setting a trap, "the taxpayer will not even need to build a corral?"

The Bureau man nodded smugly, unaware of the snare. "You're absolutely right, Mr. Murry. The mustangs won't need to be held; they'll be taken care of at once."

Something in the prison guard's manner electrified us all. I could almost smell the sparks of fire. By his very presence he still held the floor, still kept the Bureau man standing. His questions crackled. "Aha! Saving our money, are you?"

The Bureau man looked startled, and Lucius Beebe let out a "Harrrumph."

Mr. Murray snapped his next question. "Don't you know what Gomez and Burger are really after?"

The audience leaned forward to catch every syllable.

"Do you think these men give a hoot for the grazing lands?

No! They want those mustangs just to grind their flesh and bones into pet food."

I could hear the tense shuffling of boots all over the room. My heart skipped. What was coming next?

The biting voice went on, "This very day I learned that Gomez and Burger are the ones who own the rendering plant."

The audience gasped, then began muttering neighbor-to-neighbor, louder and louder.

The chairman pounded for quiet. Then he too went at the Bureau man. "Let's go back to your three hundred horses; how did you arrive at this figure?"

The man no longer had a halo; his hair was wilted dark with perspiration. He blotted it with a handkerchief. "Wh—why," he stuttered, "our men flew over in a plane and made their count. Wherever they saw one, they counted it as three."

"How's that?"

"Well . . . ll, whenever there's one, we figure two are hiding."

"Where in God's name," an irate voice boomed out, "would they hide? Our mountains are bare! Our lakes are dry! Our flatlands are treeless!"

I warmed to the man's words and to his looks. He was the postmaster of Virginia City and the spittin' image of Abraham Lincoln, but a young Lincoln, lean and dark.

Now he arched his tall frame over the aisle until he was face to face with the perspiring Bureau man. "By the beard of Tex Gladding—for that's my name—I'm here to fight this mustang slaughter."

He began fumbling in his pockets. No one interrupted him. At last he pulled out a long piece of paper. "What's more," he said, unfolding it like a road map, "I have one hundred and forty-seven signatures right here protesting this permit. Every last one of them wonders how come those two sheepmen can fence in the hull dang world for their own selves?"

The "agins" cheered loudly.

The Bureau man had a coughing spasm. "All right, all right," he agreed when the room quieted. "Suppose it is only a hundred this year. Next year it'll be two hundred. The next, four hundred, and so on. You see, Mr. Chairman, it's a matter of simple arithmetic."

This was more than the horsemen in the crowd could stomach. Their laughter rocked the courtroom, Charley's heartiest of all. He jumped up and waved to the whole room. "I'd bet my ranch against a silver dollar that every man here would go into the horse business if he could count on an increase like that."

The Bureau man ignored the interruption. "As I was saying, my job is to save the grazing land by keeping the numbers down. Pursuit by air is the humane way, and . . ."

All this while I had been waiting, waiting with my heart bursting in anger and the tears flowing inside me. Waiting for what? A vision? A picture of the long-dead mustang whose milk had given life back to my father when it was all draining away in the heat and the dust? And through my father to me? Except for her, I would not have had life. That was it! I seemed to hear that old mare whinnying for all of her kind, calling as a mare to her foal, calling, but helpless.

"Mr. Chairman!" I cried out. "If there really are too many mustangs, I agree something should be done—in a humane way. But if the pilot only wants to sell horseflesh, he doesn't care how the animal suffers. We should never allow such cruelty against living, breathing creatures that hurt and pain just like you and me!"

The Bureau man gaped around at me in open-mouthed amazement.

I pretended not to notice and went right on. "One day I followed a truckload of wild horses to the rendering plant. You should have seen them. They were torn and bleeding and only half alive. I have pictures here to prove it." And I passed my snapshots around.

"I know what the little lady means." It was Attorney Richards, who had remained quiet until now. He glanced at the pictures and passed them on. "I've seen those planes as they flush the horses out of the hills. The pilots shoot at them to panic them out into the open. By the time the animals are caught, every last one is crippled; almost dead. It's the cruelest thing imaginable."

Now big Josh Tabor, with a gold watch chain spanning his barrel of a body, stood up. He was a wealthy cowman. He swiveled around in my direction and pointed his cigar at me. "That sentimental sister doesn't understand what a mustang really is, and I propose to tell her. He's a runty, moth-eaten, mangy scrub of no value anywhere—*outside of a can of horsemeat*! He's a curse to the stockman, a nuisance to the hunter, and a pain in the neck to the Bureau of Land Management. Getting rid of him"—here he eyed me with a foxlike grin—"can be likened to a housewife's war on cockroaches in the kitchen or moths in the closet."

Gomez howled, "Yeah! Yeah! She oughta have a whole herd of the pests running in her backyard! Then see how she likes 'em!"

I started to erupt in fury, but suddenly Pa's words came back to me. "Be a girl. But think reasonable like your Pa."

Before I could answer, the man attacked me again. His tone was razor-edged. "And just what do you propose to do, young lady, when they become that numerous?"

105

"I propose . . ." I tried to keep my voice steady ". . .IF that day should come, that they be mercifully *thinned* out, not wiped out."

A ripple of applause on our side of the room.

There was a stir at the doorway behind us and a cowhand strode right up to the railing. He took off his hat and slapped it against his thigh, raising a little cloud of dust. He didn't wait for recognition; he just spoke out.

"I'm dog tired. Been de-horning and brandin' since sunup, but I knew I couldn't sleep if I didn't come to put in a word for the mustangs. They're important. They're part of the West. If we kill 'em off like these men are figgerin' to do, we kill the very critter that helped build America. The same America that gives us the right to speak here—arguing whether *they,* them mustangs, should live or die. Don't that take the cake! And we call ourselves human."

He turned and stomped out of the room, a round of cheers trailing his proud and dusty dignity.

The meeting could have ended right then, but everyone sat hushed, waiting for the other fellow to finish it off.

I remembered Mr. Harris' advice: "Let the men do it, Annie." I sighed in relief when Charley stood up. "Mr. Chairman," he said, "the supervisor of the Bureau has said that seventy-five thousand mustangs have been killed since he has been here. I propose that we save the few tough little fighters that are left. Let's respect their right to live as symbols of the old West and the freedom it stood for."

As Charley took his seat, the commissioners and the

district attorney huddled together, conferring behind their hands while the audience carried on the fight in stage whispers. Up in front, Lucius Beebe sharpened his pencil with a slim gold pocketknife, waiting for the verdict.

At last the chairman rapped for quiet. His boylike face wore its customary grin as he scanned the audience, person to person. "The Board denies this permit," he said. "The meeting is adjourned."

Wide-brimmed hats soared to the ceiling. A tribe of Paiutes or Washoes couldn't have made more noise. Boots stamped. Spurs jingled.

We had won!

12. The New Challenge

THAT NIGHT after the meeting I had a long talk
with Hobo. I couldn't help being a kid again and
talking to him the way I used to. The night was soft
and near, with one of those misty half-moons that throws a
lot of yellow light.

I found him far out in the field. He was easy to spot with
the yellow moon on his buckskin coat. His winter hair had
shed off and his hide was shiny slick.

He let me come up on him easy and slow, and being
long-legged I clambered aboard. He waited for a signal to
go, but I didn't give it. The June alfalfa was sweet and I let

him go on eating. I liked to hear him rip off a bunch of it and chew it with his big grinder teeth. He could listen and chew at the same time, which is more than some two-legged folk can do. I could tell he was listening from the way he was waggling his ears like semaphores.

"Friend Hobo," I said, leaning over so my face could rest on his neck, "you helped save a world of mustangs tonight."

The sweet grindy-chewy sound stopped. An ear swiveled my way.

"I'm mighty proud of you, Hobo. If Pa hadn't rounded you up years ago, and if you hadn't bucked me off when I was a baby, we might neither of us be here nuzzlin' in the moonlight."

Our dogs, Nip and Tucker, joined us, and were ranging in circles, sniffing good earth smells and yelping, bent on their own business. I saw the light go off in the barn and on in the kitchen. I knew that Charley would be making a pot of coffee. He was used to my night wanderings.

"Go on out and count the stars, Annie," he'd say. "It'll ready you for sleep."

But tonight I wasn't thinking of my own sleep. I was thinking of how a lot of tired mustangs in the hills could be sleeping without any fear of those murdering things from the sky.

"Hobo," I said, "you were at that meeting tonight, as sure as if you'd been sitting there on your haunches."

An owl whiffed by, and the wind made a whisper through his feathers. Neither of us shied.

"Isn't it funny, Hobo, how lovin' one horse critter can trigger off a lot of love . . . enough for all horsekind?"

I felt so good I wanted to fly. Suddenly I grabbed two fistfuls of mane, nudged Hobo in the ribs, and we flew for home, fast as wind . . . that is, fast for an old horse, and for me who hadn't barebacked in a long time.

I did sleep that night, and next morning the whole world seemed to sing. It was a bright clean decent place for living again.

The June days skipped by like happy children. Life was good. Each morning when I drove to Reno, I knew there'd be no truckload of bleeding horses ahead.

The summer bloomed and faded. October set in. And one noontime as I was crossing the bridge to return a book to the library, I spied the rangy figure of Attorney Richards coming towards me. I was glad to see him. Now I could really thank him for his help at Virginia City. The sun shone on his crinkled white hair and made the creases in his face sharp as knife edges. I noticed a pile of magazines under his arm and noticed, too, that he seemed deep in thought, and somehow sad-looking.

"Mr. Richards!" I startled him out of his daydream. "I just want to say hello and thank you for speaking up at the meeting."

The lean figure spun about. "Why, it's Annie!" he said in slow surprise. And with his free hand he shook mine the way Pa did when he called me Pardner. And there was the same look in his eye. "But why thank me?"

"Because you explained my pictures, and helped our side to win."

"But, Annie, are you satisfied with that puny victory in Virginia City?"

"Puny victory!"

"That's what it was! Nothing but a sugar pill for a big sickness. What good is it," he asked almost fiercely, "if we stop the cruel air roundups in one county? Why, the fliers and the slaughterhouses will just move on to the next. Some have already." And in the same breath he added, "You on your way to the library?"

"Yes, sir."

"Well, let's go over there so I can set down my bundle."

When we reached the wide steps he unloaded his magazines in relief. "Annie," he said, "I've been fighting for

111

years, and I know when I've won and when I got to stand up and fight again."

I could see across the river, see Mr. Harris returning to the office. I knew I should be hurrying back, too. Instead, I stood rooted. "You mean we've got to fight the whole state?"

"That's exactly what I mean. In my own time a hundred thousand mustangs have been slaughtered in Nevada alone. Today I doubt if there are twenty thousand left in all America."

I was silent, letting the truth soak in.

"The cruelty I've seen, Annie, I can't ever crowd out of my mind."

"I can't either. I dream about it nights."

"We think alike," he smiled. "Years ago, your father had the best Mustang Express around here, and you and I grew up on mustangs."

"You did? Somehow . . ." I blushed.

"Somehow what, Annie?"

"I always thought of you with books and courtrooms. Not horses."

His laughter came from deep within. "You didn't know I used to be a miner? Why, in those days I had a true mustang for a pack-and-saddle horse. Because I was a miner I named him Major. Oh, I was a wag in those days, Annie. Major was a tough little buckskin, and I was a tough young buck myself. Many's the time we split the sage and washed our faces with wind."

My mind took off. I was on Hobo, galloping bareback across the range, his mane whipping my face.

"And now when the mustang needs me," Mr. Richards was saying, "I'm not going to stand by and let people like Gomez and Burger sign his death warrant."

He slid a magazine out from the pile. "Here, look at this, Annie. Right on the cover. 'Mustang Murder!' There's enough ammunition here to shoot holes through any argument—by sheepmen, cowmen, rendering plants, or even the Bureau of Land Management. I bought every last copy."

I felt a sharp, tingling excitement. A war coming on. And here, looking right at me, was the general who would lead us to victory. Maybe he'd let me work behind the lines. Then I could keep my promise to Mr. Harris.

"I'm going to send this to each legislator." Mr. Richards was pounding the magazine with his fist. "And a fiery letter besides, just bristling with facts. And next on the docket I'll persuade Senator Slattery to sponsor a bill to stop air pursuit *everywhere* in the state. What do you say to that, Annie?"

"Wonderful! I want to help!"

"Maybe you can. I understand you type a lot of words a minute."

"Yes, sir!"

Suddenly he fell silent, And when he spoke again he seemed years older. "You see, Annie, I have to measure out my time like a miser. I don't want it running out before my work's done. Somehow I've got to get this bill through before I die."

Then he brightened. "And do you know how I'm going to do it?" He was talking more to himself than to me, and looking off into the deep purple mountains and even beyond.

I waited for him to go on.

"We must trust the people, the everyday people, Annie. We've got to believe in them. *They* are the lawmakers! You saw how it happened in Virginia City when they were aroused. Now it's got to happen in the whole state of Nevada."

I longed to say something big, to show I understood. But before I had a chance, Mr. Richards held out his hand in good-bye.

"I'm depending on you, Annie," he said, with a sparkle suddenly in his tired eyes.

I trotted on air every step of the way to the office. What an honor to be taken into the confidence of this great man. My library book was still clutched in my hand; I'd completely forgotten my errand!

The next day Mr. Richards was found dead at his desk.

13. The Mustang Bill

AND THE next thing I knew, the bundle of magazines with the "Mustang Murder" article was on my doorstep. For a long moment I didn't even stoop to pick them up. I stood looking at them, tied loosely with a piece of raveled cord, as if someone, now gone, had done it hurriedly.

I stood there afraid, feeling that I was too young, too weak to move the battle lines forward. The battle lines that the old warrior had drawn up with his last fighting breath.

"I'm depending upon you, Annie." Dear God, why had he said that? How could I break faith with this dear, dead man who had spent all of his life fighting for freedom and justice?

I remembered how he looked that day with his eyes on the faraway mountains. The mountains. "I will lift up mine eyes unto the hills, from whence cometh my help." How often Grandma Bronn had said it. Did it have true meaning? I gazed at the mountains, seeing the purple shadows upon them. And was there something walking in the shadows?

My heart began to pound. Something seemed to be speaking to me from the living shadows and across the miles of sage. Yet very intimate and close. Perhaps it was the wind that breathed a voice so gentle and strong and without words. But somehow I knew. Knew that, weak and young as I was, the battle was mine. There could be no retreating now.

Then the strength of the mountains was within me. My mind was thinking fast and clear. "We must trust the people, the everyday people, Annie. *They* are the lawmakers." Mr. Richards was right. But how could I get to them? Not a ghost of a chance. No? The idea flooded my brain.

For that ghost of a chance was a ghost writer, a person who wrote speeches and books for other people, thinking and talking just as they did. Books and speeches. Why not letters? Letters from the old dead warrior? Ghost-written, by me?

I looked again at the distant mountains. The shadows were still now, with nothing walking among them. I closed my eyes and bowed my head, with my heart crying: Thank You, out there. Oh, thank You.

Before I could write like Mr. Richards I had to learn to think like him. Every day that week I went back to the library during my lunch hour, and every time I stood there on the steps, even for a second, I could see him, white hair shining in the sun, and I could hear his voice. Then I'd run inside, and I'd hurry to the nearest table and go to work. It was exciting how I could slide over into his mind, easy as sliding into Hobo's saddle.

I found fierce joy in being Mr. Richards' ghost writer. He had cared about the wild horses, and I cared. Dead or living, we'd fight the battle together.

And so I wrote as though he were dictating: "Are you going to stuff cotton in your ears and wear blinders so you can't see and hear what's going on? So you can't see a horse chased to his death, hear the scream of the stallion, and the neighing of his mares, and the colts whinnering when a plane roars down on them?"

In our quiet Washoe Library I riffled through Mr. Richards' notes and wrote hot, racing words, and I listed the times and places where cruel, illegal roundups had taken place. That's how I spent my noon hours.

At night, Charley and I turned our kitchen into a mail room. While I typed up the letters, he printed the labels with a big black crayon and then rolled up the magazines, with my letter inside. Just before midnight we stuffed all the bundles in our saddlebags and rode off to our little postoffice in Wadsworth. Of course, I could have mailed everything in Reno the next morning, and things would have gone out just as fast. But I was never one for waiting, once a letter was licked shut. Besides, Charley and I liked jogging along in the crisp moonlight. The bigness of night, and the moon shining on the mountains, and our saddles creaking, and our horses snortin'—well, it sort of loosened up our brains so we could think free and big again.

When the last of my letters had been mailed, we knew that now someone must draw up a mustang bill. "Why don't we do it ourselves?" I asked Charley. "It'd be cheaper than hiring a lawyer."

"Sure," Charley agreed. "And we'll leave out all the whereases and heretofores."

But we were green hands at this and so we got Tex Gladding, the postmaster, to help us.

Working far into the winter nights, sometimes around our open fire and sometimes around the pot-bellied stove in the postoffice, Tex would say, "You got to work longer and harder when you're on the learning end, eh?"

One night when we seemed to be getting nowhere, I sank exhausted on our couch and covered up with Mom's warm afghan. Soon I fell asleep, and I dreamt that Mr. Richards was the great Thomas Jefferson with a copy of the American Constitution in his hands. He looked up from the print and said in a voice that went round the earth: "We the people . . ." It was so real that I awoke in startlement, with Mr. Richards' real-life words all mixed up with the Constitution. "We the people must trust the people; *they* are the lawmakers."

I grabbed a pencil and in ten minutes I wrote our bill:

> *We, the people, say it shall be unlawful for any person to hunt wild horses, mares, colts or burros by means of airborne vehicles of any kind, or motor vehicles of any kind. It shall also be unlawful to pollute water holes in order to trap such animals.*

Luckily our state senator, James Slattery, lived just up the canyon from us, and the very next evening Charley and I rode over to his ranch.

As we tied up our horses at the hitching rack, our arrival

was announced by a joyous chaos of seven barking dogs and two pups, who with much yelping and tail wagging took us to the family entrance. The door burst open, and Hi-Line, the hired man, greeted us with a wide-toothed smile. He'd earned his name because he was pretty much an expert on high-power lines.

"Come on in, folks," he drawled, leading us into a cavern of a room that somehow made us feel right at home. It was lighted only by a ruddy, spitting fire, and everywhere were signs of comfortable living—newspapers and magazines spread all about, roasted piñon nuts heaped in a bowl, a basket of apples on the mantel. And deep in a red leather chair, with his feet stretched out on a hassock, sprawled Senator James Slattery. Like some graceful tiger he untangled himself, rose up to his full six-feet-two, and welcomed us with a grip so hearty I wriggled my fingers afterward to see if they were still usable.

"Hello, neighbors!" he said in a softly rugged voice. "Come! Anchor down right here." He pushed a mess of papers off the couch, and with a grand wave of his hand invited us to sit. As we made ourselves comfortable, Hi-Line clumped in on his spiked boots and poured us the blackest coffee you ever saw.

The Senator went back to his big chair and settled in again. "My wife's in the other room fussin' over one of her animal welfare projects." He chuckled at the thought. "Would you believe it if I said we have a sow in the bathroom?"

I spoke up quickly. "Yes, I would."

"And a bunch of pigs, too?"

"Yes. I'd believe that."

"And you'd be right," he said, and he bellowed with laughter. "It beats me, Charley," he added, wiping merry tears from his eyes, "how we put up with these girls of ours who are forever gathering in the halt, the maimed, and the blind."

Charley nodded in hearty agreement.

"Right now, Kathryn's watching over Shovel-nose, our prize sow."

"*Shovel-nose!*" Charley's laughter boomed. "Why can't I think of good names like that? I'd probably have called her Droopy Ears or Curly Tail or Mrs. Grunty."

"Our son did the naming," Mr. Slattery said with a touch of pride. "He still rides her, so of course we can't have anything happen to her."

"Is she sick?" I asked.

The Senator shook his head. "Not now. But she had a hard time farrowing, and she's not the best mother in the world. Has to be watched constantly or she rolls over and crushes the little pigs."

He threw back his head and let out a meadow-lark whistle. It brought Mrs. Slattery on the run. She stood in the doorway a moment, adjusting her eyes to the dimness. She was wearing what people in storybooks would call a "tea gown," but on her feet were barn boots.

"You'll have to excuse my mixed-up appearance," she said. "Jim has probably told you of the brand-fire new little pigs. They are so absolutely adorable they'll not be going to market for a long time. Hi-Line," she called in the same breath, "why don't you bring in some of that good coffee cake?"

While the others ate and talked crops and weather, I sat restlessly stroking a cat that was smoothing his whiskers against my sleeve. I wanted to get on to the real thing! At last Mr. Slattery brought it up himself.

"Got your letter, Annie, the one about the mustangs."

I leaned forward so suddenly the cat whiffed away in fright.

"By the way, how does it feel to know you've grounded all those flyin' mustangers?"

"Oh, but we haven't! That was just a puny victory; Mr. Richards told me we've got to fight for a state law."

The Senator pulled out a big cigar, and fumbled for a match. "Did you know that he and I tried for a save-the-mustang bill last year?"

"Yes, he told me all about it, and how it died a-borning. But his last wish was to start again, and this time *win*."

"Annie feels she's got to carry on for Mr. Richards," Charley explained, pulling our precious bill out of his pocket. "The letter she wrote is the one he intended to write. And here's the bill she hopes you'll sponsor."

Without a glance at it, the Senator laid the bill face down on the table beside him.

The sudden quiet was startling. He rolled the cigar between his fingers, regarding it as if he'd never seen one before.

Then he slipped off the gold band, and leaning toward his wife, who was sitting on the hassock, he placed it on her ring finger in a kind of ceremony. Not until he'd slowly lighted the cigar and taken the first long puff did he speak. "Of course I will!" he said with conviction. "Even without reading it, I know it's right."

My mouth opened in amazement.

"Do you think Kathryn and I want to see any animals tortured? Why do you suppose we let a sow have her five little porkers in our house? But . . ." he hesitated.

"But what?" I asked.

"There'll be a lot of hurdles built up by big cattle and sheep men. You see," he went on, "the committee who must approve the bill may not be members of yours and Kathryn's humane society."

"Who will they be?"

"I don't know. Most likely it'll be the Livestock Committee, and they won't clap hands at the idea of protecting the mustangs. Come to think of it, I'll try to get it into the Public Morals Committee. They're so used to correcting injustices to people, it might have a chance there."

My heart turned a quick somersault. Again, here was a big public figure who would take on the mustang war!

"We'll all help," Charley said. "Tex Gladding and Mr. Flick and all of our neighbors."

"Yes!" I cried. "Just tell us, how do we go about it?"

Mr. Slattery didn't even have to think. "Storm the newspapers!" He clipped out his orders. "Write to every paper in the state. Get all the support you can from all the groups you can—schools, churches, clubs. The more folks who know about the plight of the mustang, the safer he'll be. Yes, sir! That letter you wrote the lawmakers, Annie, was good strong stuff. If you can get the public as stirred up as you are, maybe . . . maybe there's just a chance . . ."

I stood up to go. I could hardly wait to begin. The Slatterys stood up, too. "Come!" the Senator laughed. "You've got to see those little pigs before you hit out for home."

As I looked down at the mountain of a sow, and held one of her soft-as-silk little squealers in my hands, I knew that anyone who would protect five little pigs would surely put up a mighty battle for the mustangs.

14. Failure at Fernley

P A ALWAYS said, "Scatter enough seeds and some are bound to sprout." And that's how it was with my letters to the newspapers. Most of them probably landed in the wastebasket. But quite a few showed up in "Letters from the People" pages.

And one sprouted bigger than a sunflower. It landed on Mark Twain's battered old desk at the *Enterprise* in Virginia City. Lucius Beebe sat there now, with the old six-gun still hanging handy above it, and he made that desk roar as it used to roar in the old days when Twain had his dander up, spitting daggers and brimstone, fighting for something worthwhile.

"Don't shoot the horses!" Beebe shouted. *"Shoot a legislator!"* The words burst from him like steam. "What have the wild horses done to deserve butchery and mass extinction? The mustangers who make a living at it are savages. They enjoy being filth at five cents a pound for live horseflesh!"

Beebe couldn't stem the flow of his words. He didn't want to! He rolled up his sleeves and shook his fist at the injustice. "Passenger pigeons," his stub of a pencil growled, "used to darken the heavens with their numbers. They and the buffalo were slaughtered by the millions. For what? For blood money, that's what! The American people will never recover from the shame of it!

"Man!" He spat out the word. "I rightly believe animals are his superior. Man is the only thing on earth where the supply exceeds the demand. How can he justify his existence?"

Now his voice rose to its fullest boom. "We at the *Enterprise* demand passage of the mustang bill. The only opposition it can possibly provoke is greed, brutality, and a total contempt for wildlife."

I was all out of breath when I finished reading the thunderous roar of Lucius Beebe. I couldn't wait for Pa to hear it, so on my way home I read it to him and Mom in their steamy-warm kitchen. When I had done, Pa jumped up, almost upsetting his plate of corned beef and cabbage. He was waving his arm like he had a flag in it.

"Rings like the Bible!" he said in awe. "Or like elegant swearing!"

The word spread. In the heart of our cattle country, a

ninety-year-old cowboy got his say-so into the Elko paper, in spite of their bitter stand against us.

As a little string-bean boy, he'd watched wild mustangs paw and roll in waterholes.

"It was dumbfounding," he said, "to see what their pawin' and rollin' did. No masons could of sealed that bottom better. Why, it'd hold water until late summer. And in winter when snow piled deep, many's the time I watched the horses paw and uncover feed for other animals as well as theirselves. Even their manure scatters seed and richens the land. Them mustangs ought to be kept, not kilt."

I saved that letter. It sounded so much like the things Pa used to tell me about horses.

Everywhere but in Reno, the papers took a stand. Here they kept silent as mice, except for my friend Lura Tularski. She dug into the history of the horse and made the mustang as important to America as George Washington. Her column kept up a running chatter of questions and answers. How is the Quarter Horse able to beat the fastest Thoroughbred for a quarter of a mile? How can he outdash a motorcycle? How does it happen he can twist and swerve and spin on his hocks to make the best cowpony in the world? Where did he get his short back, his sturdy legs, his little fox ears? From the mustang! From the mustang! Week in, week out, she proved that mustang blood gave swiftness and stamina to the Quarter Horse, to the Morgan, to the Saddlebred, to all American breeds.

But in spite of everything, the war grew bitter. The enemy grew stronger. The skies roared with black-market roundups. Yet even in the darkest hours I had only to gaze upon the wide sweeping plains, the walking shadows on the mountains, the meadow of bright stars at night to know again why freedom was worth the fight. Even on that day when I learned the U. S. Wildlife Service couldn't help.

Kindly as he could, the big square-built government man said, "Try to understand, Miss Annie. Since the mustangs were once domesticated, they are not considered wild, like birds and fish and buffalo. So for that reason—although running free for generations—they do not qualify for protection under our Wildlife Service. It's crazy, I know; but that's the way the law sees it." Even on that lost day, I would not let myself give up.

One late afternoon when I felt the mustangers were closing in on me, a stranger suddenly appeared at the office. I looked up and there he was, a swarthy mountain of a man. His eyes kept darting right and left so that I seemed to be looking at the whites of his eyes, never really seeing into the man.

In a voice like a smothered foghorn he mumbled his name, quickly adding, "If you ever squeal on me, I'm dead." And with his hand he made a slash across his throat.

I shook my head, too frightened to speak.

"I'm a truck driver. I haul mustangs to the rendering plants," he croaked in his foghorn voice. "If I don't move 'em, somebody else will," he explained with shame and confusion in his darting eyes.

And still I couldn't speak. He leaned over farther until I could feel his breath in my face.

"I got my orders to pick up a load of mustangs tomorrow. At Fernley, near your ranch. They're there now. Dead-beat and thirsty. If it's evidence you want . . . But Jees, if you ever squeal on me . . ."

My hands were trembling, but my voice was steady. "I've just named you Zeke," I said. "I didn't hear your real name, but I'll never forget your help."

Like a lumbering bear he was out of the office, and gone.

That night I raced for home. We had to work fast. Charley and I both knew the spot at Fernley. We used to check it often for captured horses. But since the meeting at Virginia City the place had been deserted as a graveyard.

We didn't bother about our own supper. We filled our old pickup truck with hay and buckets of water, and drove out the ditch road, with the canal yawning on one side and the Truckee on the other.

It was dark night, wild with wind, and only the car lights to probe the blackness. They showed up the rutted road and the rabbit brush that grew rank alongside. We traveled slow, trying to keep the racket down. Then at a bend our lights caught the corral, and there were the horses . . . huddled in a furry bunch, rumps to the wind. The wind swished their tails and lifted their manes, and the only sound was the wind.

As we drove closer they spooked, shying on legs as stiff as fenceposts. You could see their eye-whites and hear their snortings. Even as we tossed our hay over the fence they couldn't trust us. We were man, the enemy. We smelled like mustangers.

We set down our buckets, one in each corner, then we backed the truck away so the horses could eat and drink in peace. We turned off the car lights and played our flashlight over the bunch, watching them tear at the hay, fight over it.

"I count fifty-three head," Charley said, focusing his light on a crippled mare too weak to struggle.

"Charley!" I cried. "You've got your wire cutters. Let's cut the fence!"

"No," he said with slow and bitter contempt. "We don't dare! The horses are on private property. We don't know how they were rounded up or where. And——"

I clutched his arm. "Listen! I hear a truck!"

"Shut your door, Annie. Quick, before there's trouble."

Instead, I grabbed my camera and jumped out. Before Charley could stop me, I scrambled onto the roof of the cab and lay there flat and still, waiting my chance. Scarce breathing, I screwed in a flash bulb. I watched a big truck turn in, maneuver in the narrow road, then back up to the corral. I heard the tailgate slam down, heard the guttural voices of the men. Now, a lasso swung out and looped the crippled mare, tumbling her heels over head, and dragging her up the ramp.

This was my picture! I stood up, splay-legged for balance. I snapped, and reloaded, and the lasso went out again. It missed its mark! The truck was rolling now, tailgate dragging. It was coming toward us! My flash had given us away. It was going to hit!

I fell flat on the roof, gripping with my fingernails, waiting for the crash. Then I saw a glint of metal below. Charley was leaning out the window and his six-shooter spoke the old persuasive language of the West. The driver understood. He made a sharp swerve, just clearing our bumper. Limp as a dead fish I slid onto the bed of the truck. Charley gunned the motor and we were off.

We had our evidence, but it would not help the fifty-three mustangs that would soon be dead and canned.

15. "Wild Horse Annie"

AFTER OUR failure at Fernley, I didn't go out to see Hobo that night, or for days. I was bowed down with shame and helplessness, and I couldn't shake free of my deep disappointment.

I remembered one time when Hobo got a mean gash across his chest from running into a barbed wire fence, and the vet came, and he put a lip twitch on him. The pinching rope and the long stick dangling from his muzzle worried Hobo so much that he paid no mind to the sharp needle pulling the wound together. That's the way it was with me. My days at the office were like wearing a twitch. I was so busy I couldn't feel the big pain still burning inside me.

But the moment I got into my car and was all alone I felt failure pressing against my throat, my chest; I could hardly breathe. Even the mountains that I loved seemed to close in on me, and I thought about the wild ones hidden in their folds. I imagined I could see shapes of them, dancing in the dust, zigzagging from ledge to ledge. At the slightest rumble in the sky, I'd pull off the road and look up. I had to know if it was a big passenger ship, or a small plane spitting buckshot into the shadows.

And so a week went by, and not a word from Senator Slattery. And another week. And then one night when I was washing up the supper dishes and I'd just persuaded Charley to ride over to the Slatterys with me, the telephone rang, sharp with insistence.

"Must be long distance," Charley said. "You better answer."

With soapy hands I reached for the phone. It was long distance all right. Carson City calling.

"Annie!" came the Senator's resounding voice. "Two pieces of news for you, young lady."

"Oh?"

"The bill went to the right committee—the Public Morals group. They'll give us as good a chance as we could hope."

I found my voice. "Fine! And what else?" I asked eagerly.

"The Humane Society is trying to help." There was a chuckle in his tone.

"Why, that's wonderful!"

"It ought to be, but it's giving us problems. They're worried about too many things."

"Like what?"

"They're moaning about the use of chickens and rabbits as pets, and they're even suggesting protection for coyotes and prairie dogs! By comparison, it makes the wild horse seem so big and brawny he doesn't need our help. How about your coming to the hearing tomorrow?"

I went, all the way to Carson City, even though I had the payroll to get out and could stay only an hour. But that hour was long enough for a lot to happen. It gave me something new to fight for, and with. A new name!

As I entered the stately senate chamber, I could feel an expectant hush like at a play before the curtain goes up. People were already in their seats—cowmen and sheepmen, giving off their warm, earthy smells; and welfare ladies, some pretty and buxom, some lean as a flagpole; and reporters with pencils behind their ears; and the committee, solemn as owls. As I crawled over knees to find a seat, the little man from the Bureau, the one with the duck-fuzz hair, spoke out in a stage whisper loud enough to wake the dead: "Well . . . ll . . . ll, if it isn't Wild Horse Annie!"

"Yeah! Yeah!" Al Trivelpiece, a reporter, took up the cry: "Here comes Wild Horse Annie! Wild Horse Annie!"

Something in me wanted to explode. I wanted to yell back at the Bureau man, "*You!* You're nothing but duck fuzz! And *you,* Mister Trivelpiece, *your name suits!*" But all of a sudden I felt hotly proud to be called Wild Horse Annie. Proud, I tell you! And I was about to tell them so when the meeting was rapped to order.

The first person called upon was a tiny woman, delicate as a teacup. Her mission was to put an end to Easter brutality—rabbits dyed purple and twirled about by their ears, and chicks colored pink and sold as pets to youngsters who squeezed them to death.

Someone in the room laughed, but I couldn't laugh. I was back in our kitchen, a very little girl, holding in my hand a fluff of yellow that had hatched itself in my pocket. No, I couldn't laugh. I was closer to tears, remembering the beady shining eye and how I breathed on the little thing with half a breath, and the fluff was too wetly new to stir.

A restless audience tore me from my memory. Coughs and harrumphs all around, chairs creaking, boot-heels scraping, heads turning to the clock on the wall. I glanced too. My time was running out. Much as I sympathized with the woman and her concern, I was anxious to get on to the mustang bill.

With only fifteen minutes left for me, a solid, towering man stood up. He had a nose, large and long and blunt. Grandma called noses like his a mark of intelligence; they got that way from poking into many books and other matters of true importance. And so it was. He asked for recognition and it was promptly granted.

Then, as if there were all the time in the world, he coolly took a watch from his vest and checked it against the wall clock.

"Mr. Chairman," he said in a quiet, controlled voice, "time is of the essence. We are here to talk about a bill to prohibit mechanized roundups of wild horses, and I wish to cite a pertinent incident." He paused just long enough to make everyone wonder what in the world it could be. And still he didn't tell us.

"This incident," he said, "should convince anyone in this room who is teetering on the fence of indecision."

There was a respectful silence throughout the chamber.

"As a lawyer," he went on, "I am now handling a case for a client who has three young daughters. They in turn have three horses who have won enough blue ribbons to delight the soul of three little girls."

The quiet controlled voice made an icy correction. "That is," he said, "they *had* three horses." Then his anger burst and his face went purple-red. "Those horses," he exploded, "were rounded up by plane and truck and sold to a slaughter-house to be stuffed into a can."

There was a buzzing sound all around the room. In the commotion I had to leave. Payrolls wouldn't wait. They meant groceries for hungry children.

But within the week I had news. As I turned onto the ditch road for home one evening, I saw Charley waving me in. "Long distance from Carson City!" he yelled, making a megaphone of his hands. "Hurry!"

I ran to the house and gulped a breathless hello into the mouthpiece.

"Annie?" It was Mr. Slattery's voice, but it wasn't big and booming and friendly. It was dry and husky, like the sound a pine cone makes when it rolls downhill and hits rock. "Annie," he repeated, "listen carefully."

The words came fast now, to get them over with. "The committee will recommend passage of your bill, if . . ."

He paused, and I could feel my heart thumping against my ribs.

"If," he said, "it leaves to the government men the right to hunt wild horses by plane and truck."

My mind raced back to my afternoon visit with the Bureau man. "But, Mr. Slattery," I cried, "if they thought the grazing land was being hurt, they could kill off every single mustang."

"I know."

"And, Mr. Slattery, with so much of Nevada being public land, our bill will cover such a tiny part."

"No need to tell me, Annie. I've been tumbling it over in

my mind until I'm dizzy. How can a flyer see boundary lines across a desert? How can he know when he's over public land or private land?"

"He'll make his own boundaries," I said, "just where he wants them."

"Exactly! And how can a sheriff who's trying to enforce our law tell whether a flyer is hunting stray sheep for a ranch, or wild horses for a rendering plant? Or, for that matter, stealing pet horses?"

I remembered the three horses that had belonged to the three little girls. And I thought of Hobo, and what might happen to him if this dreadful murder went on.

I was all mixed up in my mind. "What *can* we do, sir?"

"It's up to you, Annie."

"What would *you* do?" I asked, trying to hang onto his coattails, trying to reach for help.

"It's your bill, Annie. But I warn you, the Bureau won't budge. They insist that federal land be excluded. After all, they represent the national government, and we can't fight Washington in Carson City."

My heart sank. "Is it that serious?" I asked.

"I'm afraid it is. The big ranchers are bringing a lot of pressure on the men in Washington. Most folks back east probably don't know—or care—about the mustangs way out here in Nevada."

"But they're Americans. The mustangs belong to them, too."

"I know—but . . ."

"Well, what would you do?" I insisted, pleading again for help.

There was so dead a silence I almost shrieked, "Are you still there?"

The words came reluctantly. "If it were up to me, Annie, I'd agree to the Bureau's demand."

"Agree!" I nearly choked on the word.

"Half a loaf is better than none, Annie. Remember how many attempts have failed. Are you going to let it die again? Think it over. Talk it over with Charley, and call me back."

I hung up. I could feel the tears running down my face and I couldn't stop them. Charley took my hand and pulled me over to the big old chair that faced the fire. We could both squeeze into it with our skinny cowboy hips and have room left over for our littlest dog, who promptly joined us.

"All those stamps we bought!" I sobbed. "And my new secondhand typewriter. So much money!" I buried my face in Charley's neck and wept.

When I quieted a little, he took out his bandanna and mopped my face and his own neck. "It's all right, little one. Hush a moment, and listen to me. *Look like a girl. Cry like a girl. But think like your Pa!*"

At mention of Pa I blubbered all the more. Then in the middle of a sob I suddenly burst into laughter. "He'd say," I snuffled, " 'Comes a time you got to horse-trade.' "

16. Stockings Hung by the Fire

HORSE-TRADING isn't much fun when you know you've been taken in. As soon as we agreed to the Bureau's demand, the bill passed lightning-quick. The newspapers cheered as if the mustangs were now and forever safe. Lucius Beebe splashed the verdict as a great victory. My friend Lura called it THE MUSTANGS' TRIUMPH.

Even California papers hailed Senator Slattery and me as guardians of the wildlife. They all said pretty much the same thing: That the first shot in the mustang war had been fired in a little courtroom in Storey County and now the second volley was ringing around the whole great state of Nevada.

I felt no such joy. I said to Senator Slattery: "We've won but we've lost."

"Look here, Annie," he scolded, "you've done what Mr. Richards tried for years to do. You've planted the first footprint on the trail."

He didn't come right out and say, *Now you've got to go on*. I knew, though, that's what he meant. But I was tired, so tired. I didn't think I could fight any more. I just wanted to crawl under a rock like a lizard, and stay there asleep until the summer sun baked me awake.

Nothing helped. The mountains stood stark and bare. The wind moaned wearily. Even with Charley, I felt so utterly small and alone. "I'm depending on you, Annie." Mr. Richards' words weighted my shoulders, heavied my heart.

Wearily I went to work and wearily came home. I bought our groceries in little off-beat stores where I knew no one, and I hurried out with only the bare necessities, so anxious was I to escape congratulations I didn't deserve.

I didn't want to see anyone, not even the friends who had helped. Charley and I stopped going to church. We stayed away from the square dances. We didn't want to run into Tex Gladding or Mr. Flick, or the lawyer for the three little girls whose horses had been slaughtered. I was too tired to care who won that case. The horses were gone forever. Nobody could help them now.

The only happy time in my day was just before supper. Charley would saddle up, and for a whole wonderful hour we breathed the smell of sage and pine, and I'd be laughing at the snorting joy of Hobo and the antics of Nip and Tucker. Sometimes we'd stop by and watch Mr. Graf training his Appaloosey on a lunge line. And sometimes he rode along with us, almost in silence, each of us tossing his cares to the winds.

Full of peace, we came home to our supper by campfire, and afterward Charley played his harmonica until we both grew sleepy.

But the moment my head touched the pillow I came wide awake, and the nagging guilt of failure plucked at my brain. When I did sleep, I dreamed of an ocean of water and I was trapped underneath a raft with my clothes snagged on the underside of it and I was drowning, holding my breath until my lungs were ready to burst. Kicking, suffocating, I woke up drenched in sweat. And I'd rush to the window for air. And I'd cry out, "O God, let somebody else take over. They've beaten me, beaten me." I looked up to the stars, but they were hopelessly far away; cold, pitiless, without answer.

My birthday came, and Mom sent a big cake over to the office. It had chocolate mustangs bucking all over the snow-white frosting, and on a pennant stuck in it were the words: WILD HORSE ANNIE. They were a stab.

Poor Mom! She did her best to cheer me up. But I was no longer the child she could comfort with a hug and a sweet; no longer the child whose burden she could share. The battle was mine alone.

December came in, and Christmas week, and with it days of hard, cold rain. It pinged against the windows; and on the mountain slopes it pried the snow loose and shoved it into the Truckee River. What was once an innocent stream became a raging torrent, bursting from its bed, sprawling over the land. It sprawled around the Double Lazy Heart, flooding the barn and the fields and making an island of our house.

With true mustang sense Hobo rounded up our five horses and drove them onto the little rise near the railroad bridge. Through the window we could watch them, all huddled to-

gether, rumps against the wind. I felt proud of Hobo, like a mother whose wild son shows good horse sense. Charley had long ago built a shelter there on the high ground, and at the first radio warning he had stocked it with hay.

But I, in my numbness, had neglected our cupboard. And here with the calendar saying Merry Christmas we were marooned with no roast, no turkey, only a big elderly duck that had been hit by a jeep weeks ago. Charley had dressed it and put it in the deep freeze against need.

"One thing sure," he laughed, "today's the need!"

All Christmas morning we roasted it and laid strips of bacon across its bony breast, and we basted and basted it. And all morning, and half the afternoon, there was this delicious fragrance of browning duck steaming through the house until we could hardly wait to taste its goodness. The dogs, too, were drooling and waltzing around the stove on their hind legs, snuffing in the good smells, yelping in eagerness.

Dinnertime came and my testing fork couldn't pierce the duck's hide. Yet how magnificent it looked on the platter with squiggles of mashed potatoes around it and shredded carrots. I had made a table bouquet of some Everlastings. The flowers were bright as new-picked ones—yellows and blues and orange and rose.

"Looks like a party!" Charley nodded.

"It is!" I gasped, staring out the window at the rain-draggled parade of Eli Pike followed by Mrs. Pike holding a new baby, and all the older Pike children each holding a younger one in hand.

I flung wide the door and gathered them in, wet and dripping, all making little rivers on the bare floor.

Mrs. Pike's eyes were red-rimmed. "We're flooded out," she said. "Eli," she hesitated, "Eli thought maybe you . . ."

"You bet we will!" shouted Charley.

Back went the duck into the oven to be kept warm, and out came towels and blankets and sweaters. Then all the grown-ups fell to undressing the little ones and wrapping them up, and in no time Charley's fire was roaring and we'd stretched a lineful of dripping dresses and shirts and pants and socks in front of the fire.

"Why, it's a real Christmas!" I cried "Stockings hung by the fire with care."

"But nothing in 'em," a little Pike said, his face puckered up for crying.

"Just you wait and see! They've got to dry out first."

It was hard to tell who was helping whom. Such laughter and talking all at the same time.

"Oh, look at Pa!" Emma and Clara, young ladies now, were screeching with laughter. "Pa's drowning in Charley's pants."

Mrs. Pike and I joined in the laughter. We were working like a team. With safety pins and string we made dresses out of bath towels. Even the boys had to wear dresses. And Charley's socks, darned and undarned, made warm footgear.

At last when heads were rubbed dry and faces shone with rubbing, we brought out the duck, none the worse for the delay. And the potato squiggles were browned prettier than ever now.

Who minded a tough drumstick or a wing or a stringy slice of breast when there was enough for all, and giblet gravy so brown and good, and dressing to melt in your mouth?

When we were filled to bursting, Mrs. Pike wiped her baby's mouth and turned to Charley and me. "How do you keep so happy, you two? It's the remarkablest thing I ever, ever see."

Charley and I looked at each other in surprise. "It's

Annie," he said quietly. "She keeps me happy with her crusadin' and all the work she piles on me."

Mrs. Pike still wasn't satisfied. "Annie," she said, her eyes beginning to flood, "but how come *you* are so happy, even with us eatin' you outa house and home, and the river at your door."

I was thinking of the stockings drying and how to fill them, and I remembered some bead belts our weekend children had started. They weren't quite finished, but the Pike children could work on them. It'd be something to do while Charley and I hauled out the sleeping bags and . . .

"Annie!" Eli Pike said. "Ma's right. You allus seem right up on the bit, and lively as a colt. Someway you musta struck a rich vein o' gumption from somewheres."

"I'm not always this happy," I admitted. "But tonight you folks came and made me feel needed."

"Tell more, Annie," Charley said softly.

I knew what he meant. And so with most of the children listening but some falling asleep, I began Grandma's story.

"Our wagon rolled through dust. A choking, sneezy wilderness of dust . . ."

17. At Black Rock Desert

THE FLOOD waters dried. January froze and thawed. February wore itself out. And the Pikes wouldn't have believed how gloomy I felt, marking time, doing nothing, my job unfinished, but not knowing where to turn. Then one early evening in March my gloom vanished in a flash.

I was alone in the office. I had stayed after five to prepare a special report for Mr. Harris. Time slid away and before I knew it, the whole building had that night-empty feeling. Suddenly in the enormous quiet I heard the click of the mail-slit, then a lisp of sound as an envelope skidded across the floor. I ran to pick it up, and with a sense of impending excitement read:

Mis WILD HORSE ANNIE
PERSONNAL

The paper inside was lined wide apart, like the tablets we had in first grade, and the printed letters were scrawled in a childlike hand. Street sounds seemed far away . . . only the clock on the wall ticking as loud as my heart. In the silence I read the note and I could hear Zeke's foghorn voice saying the words he had so painstakingly printed:

DEAR ANNIE:
   BLACK ROCK DESERT — NORTH
OF PYRAMID LAKE, ROUNDUP
TOMORROW — EARLY.

                ZEKE

I knew what must follow. It was almost as if I had been expecting this. I memorized the directions. I would be there. Alone. I locked the letter in my top drawer. If anything should happen to me, my desk would be searched. They'd know where and why I'd gone. Someone would tell Charley.

I brushed the thought away. Hastily I wrote on Mr. Harris' scratch pad: "Must be gone all morning. Will explain later." I tilted the pad against his ash tray where he'd surely see it the first thing.

The next morning I stole out of bed at two and left a note for Charley. "Sleepyhead!" I said. "Don't you know morning hours have gold in their mouth? Which reminds me we are out of toothpaste! Your early bird is on her way . . ." I started to say where, but quickly stabbed a period instead. Charley could not be told. The mustangers might shoot a man, but they wouldn't shoot me.

In the half light of dawn, Black Rock Desert looked desolate and lonely, a waste place of the earth. Once it had been an inland sea, hundreds of feet deep. Now years of sun and wind had baked it into hardpan, hard and gray as marble. It was mottled like marble too, with cracks crisscrossing it. Around this dry crust of earth scraggly sagebrush grew, and old volcanic rocks were piled higgledy-piggledy. As there was no sign of rain, I hid my car in a dry wash where sage grew on either side. Old and dusty as it was, it blended into the landscape like a chameleon.

Then I slung my camera over one shoulder, my field glasses over the other, and feeling of the pistol in my belt, I scrambled along the rim until I reached a benchland that boasted the only juniper for miles. Here I took my stand. I could see out over the dead-level tableland without, I hoped, being seen.

In all this wilderness I felt little as a lost baby field mouse. I crouched motionless, quivering with cold and fear. Even the sky looked cold. It was the color of pewter with not a bird in sight. A desert-swift fox with a pocket rat in his mouth circled my tree. He glanced at me with his yellow eyes and padded noiselessly on his way. I looked at my watch. Only ten minutes had passed.

Suddenly a high, thin *Whi-eeeee* cut into the stillness. I reached for my pistol, certain I'd been discovered. But it was just a ground squirrel, sitting up on his haunches, his tiny paws crossed over his belly. He sat there frozen, except for a little twitch to his whiskers. After he scurried away I felt even more alone, and I was glad when the first brightness of the sun struck the Granite Range and warmed the world.

I thought of home. Charley would be reading my note now. Would he guess it had something to do with the mustangs? My knees were shaking and my teeth still chattering. Then I heard a whirring sound overhead. I swung my binoculars to the sky and caught a flock of ducks on their way south to Pyramid Lake.

More long moments of stillness. Time to think. In all this barrenness where is the dotted line that marks off the government lands? And who owns all that blueing sky above? Then from far away a motor's drone! And out of the hills in the distance a wispy cloud flirting along a ledge. It *could be* dust kicked up by fast-running mustangs. *It is!*

A plane is diving, banking, whipping them into line. Look! As they gallop onto the tableland, one escapes to the north! Two are kiting off to the south. The plane roars, is everywhere at once—swooping like a hawk, chasing the loners back into the bunch.

Now it flies away over their heads. I hear a spitfire of shots. Then more strays join the band. Together they are flying across the desert. On they come. In single file! Toward *me!* I can hear the thunder of their hoofs pounding the earth.

Now a nearer noise! It drowns out hoofbeats, drowns out the roar of the plane. Trucks, two of them, are rumbling out onto the desert floor. A man is standing up on the bed of one. He's strapped to a post. His arms are free, free to twirl a rope. He's spinning it wide. He's warming up for the throw!

The horses are coming in closer and closer, trying to

escape the plane, but now the truck takes up the chase! Like a long snake uncoiling, the rope whangs through the air. It catches the neck of a crazed stallion. Instantly the truck veers, jerking the horse's head back, yanking him completely around and upside down. Through my glasses I see him—a splashy-marked pinto. I see his eye-rolling fear, and the blood spilling from his nostrils. He's up again, fighting with all the heart in him. He runs away with the rope! He thinks he's free! But as he runs he pulls a frightening thing from the bed of the truck—a huge tire. It bounces and bounds after him, a living monster.

Bucking and plunging, he drags it through the dust, fighting, fighting, fighting to be free. He almost runs away with it! But a second rope snakes through the air, lassoes him clear back to the shoulder, and a second tire comes bumping

after him. With a last burst of energy he lugs his two anchors until the weight of them pulls the ropes tighter and tighter around his neck, choking off his breath. He staggers a few paces, and stops, head bowed in defeat. It has taken four men, a couple of hundred-pound tires, and two giant machines to quench his spirit.

My heart all but exploding in anger, I looked on, helpless. Suddenly I remembered my pistol. My hand touched it, but what could one pistol do against a whole gang? It was no use. My only weapon was my camera.

I was no longer afraid. Boldly I stood up and snapped my pictures. My hands were icy-cold and steady as I snapped again and again, and again. I would have my evidence. I must!

Standing in plain sight now, I watched aghast as mare after mare was choked to the ground until the desert floor was blotched with blood and heaving bodies.

Only one little mustang was left. A splay-legged colt. His herd instinct was strong, but he was dazed. Should he stay with the bunch, lying all over the desert, or should he bolt for the hills? Wait! The noose is sailing toward him. It's going to catch him. He shoots up like a rocket, his toothpick legs raking the air. He bounds out of reach . . . but he's heading for the truck!

Something snapped in my mind. With flooding horror I realized that I was seeing a nightmare version of the old hospital painting. The colt was my little Buck. Mine to catch, to gentle. . . . Suddenly I found myself screaming: "Run away, you little brown bullet! Run. Run. Run!" I covered my mouth to stop my screaming.

In the turmoil and excitement the mustangers did not hear me. They were laughing hoarsely. "No meat on his bones . . .weighs no more'n a flea. Let 'im go." It was the voice of Zeke!

And still the colt hovered near the bunch, smelling for his mother, watching while she was loaded. I watched, too, saw forefoot tied to hindfoot, then the half-dead mare dragged up the ramp and slung aboard. And more horses loaded. And more. Pushed, jolted, prodded to their feet, body crushed against body, until the truck was full.

At last the tailgate slammed shut. In the other truck men were carefully coiling ropes, stacking the tires neatly, one atop the other. Then both trucks rolled off into the sunlit morning, carrying the horses toward death.

I was alone now in the desert. Alone, except for a little left-over broomtail who gave one baby-nicker in the direction of the trucks. Then all in an instant he grew up. With a snorty shake of his head he high-tailed it for the far, far mountains. I watched him go, kicking up a ragged tail of dust behind him, watched until he was lost in the cloud of his own making. Then the cloud, too, was gone.

"You're home free!" I cried fiercely, and fell sobbing in the sand.

18. Found—a Champion

PA WAS at home. He was out back mending harness for some child who'd been given a pony cart. He'd had his lunch and was smoking his pipe. And there was such a look of happiness and peace about him that it started softening my hurt. He looked up at me, and a smile of pleasure spread across his face. Then he saw that I had been crying and he began treating me just the way he used to when I was a little kid with a skinned knee. He would wash all around the wound with warm sudsy water, not coming anywhere near the bleeding part for a long, long time.

Now he was doing the same thing. As his needle curved in and out of the leather, he began talking all around my hurt.

"Pardner!" he said. "I'd bet my last sack o' tobacco you couldn't guess what I been cogitating on."

He expected no answer. I sat down on my heels, and began rubbing the palms of my hands where my fingernails had dug in. Pa acted like he never noticed my hands or my red swollen eyes or the desert dust all over my skirt. He kept on working while he spoke.

"This morning," he said, "I was barrelin' along from the Douglas place with a load of wool, and seemed like I was the only critter alive in the hull world. I could see mile on mile, clean acrost to the Bear Lodge Mountains, and not so much as a fly between me and the Almighty. Nothin' but earth and sky and a blue shimmer over the hull thing."

I felt a warm sense of peace, watching Pa work.

"Y'know, Annie, I got to thinkin' why Nevada folks is bigger'n most."

"Why, Pa?"

"Wal, a man's got to think twice afore comin' to this lonesome, empty land to live. But when he does, he's purty much a man! Leastwise, most of 'em is."

I thought of the mustangers and my skin ran prickly up the back of my neck.

"I said, *most* is!" Pa repeated. "Most of us love the lonesomeness. And because they're so few of us, we're all on the same footin'. Take, f'rinstance, when I gets to town this noon I meets up with an Injun from Nixon. Now he's got a right to hate every dang white man in the world, ain't he?"

I nodded.

"Instead, we enjoyed a pipe together behind the old Post Office. And then guess who I meets?"

"Who?" I asked. In school we'd been taught to say "whom" but Mom told me when you're with Pa, it's like being in Rome. You got to talk his language.

Pa was still trying to cheer me up, to ease my hurt. He broke into a great roar of laughter. "Why, I runs spang into Congressman Baring! Now name me another state where you got only one Congressman in Washington and you kin call him Walt, and pass the time a day with him like he was just any old cowpoke."

Pa snapped the leather to test the stitches he'd made. Satisfied that they held, he went on.

"Baring's a man with an eye as deep and gentle as a doe's. And he's got shoulders mountain-big, and that's as it ought to be 'cause he carries a lot o' worry on 'em."

Pa carefully put his needle away in a box. The harness was neatly mended now and so was my heart. I went over to him and kissed his warm leathery cheek.

"Child, child," he said very softly, "I know somethin's hurtin' you deep down and you'd rather not talk about it. Remember," he chuckled, "we're blood-fed by the milk of a long-ago mustang. An' that gives us somethin' extry to fight with."

I was scarce surprised next morning when Mr. Baring strode into the office. He came often to see Mr. Harris when he was in Reno.

I thought, Pa's right. Mr. Baring is not just a name in the paper or a picture on a poster. He's a friend. *My* friend! My very own voice in Washington.

I heard him say a pleasant good morning to Ruthie at the switchboard, and as he walked down the aisle to Mr. Harris' office he stopped by my desk. "Had a good chat with your Dad yesterday," he said. "He's mighty proud of you, Annie. As for Charley . . . well, he's taken the place of the son he lost."

A whole flood of memories washed over me, then something inside made me jump up. "Mr. Baring!" I almost shouted. "How soon do you go back to Washington?"

"Next week, Annie."

Suddenly I was speechless. There was a long silent moment before he asked, "Anything I can do for you?"

"Oh, yes!" Catching my breath I said, "It's about the mustangs, sir. The air roundups are still going on. Those men want to grind up every last one. Soon there won't be any left! Can't you do something in Washington?"

Mr. Baring sat down in the customer chair beside my desk. He picked up my glass paper weight with the little

forest of trees inside. He shook it intently and made a snow flurry as if he hoped to find the answer there. A fire siren wailed in the distance, and a box elder bug crawled slowly along my desk. Finally he said, "Nevada has a reputation as a gambling state. Our citizens are rough, rugged men. But everyone knows that deep down there is a core of tenderness." His face creased into a sudden smile. "Saving the wild horses, Annie, might be proof to the world."

I waited in suspense.

Then he began to question himself. "But with all our economic worries and our foreign problems, it won't be easy to arouse interest in the vanishing mustang."

"But we've *got* to do something!" I insisted. "You're the only one who can."

He stood up, and out of his deep kindliness he said, "Suppose you write me the whole story, Annie. Give me the mustang's role in history. Give me figures on mustang population, say, fifty years ago and now. Present both sides of the picture, honestly—the need to conserve the range and the need to save the horses. Then, Annie, end up with a sound solution. After I have all this ammunition, I'll write a bill." He hit my desk with his fist. "By thunder, I'll write a bill that will make airborne roundups as criminal as treason."

I seized his hand and wrung it as if we'd already won. Again I had found someone big to champion the mustang's cause.

19. The Power of Children

THIRTY DAYS and thirty-two pages later a bulky package, plastered all over with special delivery and airmail stamps was on its way from the Double Lazy Heart to Congressman Baring in Washington.

For two weeks there was no word. Each day I waited in growing tension for the mail. At ten-thirty in the morning my eye was on that slit in the door like a cat at a mousehole. Once I even made the postman rummage deep in his bag to see if he had overlooked an important letter from Washington.

I wanted so terribly to bring good news home to Charley. He had developed a cough, a kind of wheeze, like horses have when their hay is dusty. All of Mom's favorite homemade remedies did no good. We tried lemon juice mulled with honey, and steaming camomile tea, and goose-grease rubbed on his chest and kept smelly-hot with a red woolen stocking. Nothing helped.

Finally we called on good old Doctor Obermeyer in his crowded office with bottles and jars all over the walls. He diagnosed the cough as a kind of bronchitis.

Charley laughed in gay good humor. "*Bronc*-itis!" he repeated. "I'm surprised it's not mustang-itis!" He seemed enormously relieved, almost pleased by the verdict.

While Charley was dressing, the doctor called me aside. He was a little cricket of a man and wore gold-rimmed glasses that kept sliding down his nose. He spoke slowly, gravely, looking dead ahead, trying to keep his glasses in place.

"It's a condition of the lungs," he explained, "in which they refuse to bellow in and out normally. They just can't take in enough oxygen."

I listened, rigid. Unbelieving.

"But it could be a year or several years, Annie, before Charley's lungs actually fail. Meanwhile," the kindly voice said, "live those years richly."

The doctor's telephone buzzed then and I could tell from his clipped orders that it was an emergency. I stepped out of the office with questions whirling through my mind, but knowing in my heart that nobody on earth could answer them.

Charley and I went on with our life. We got a boy to help in the fields. At first Charley bristled. "We don't need help! What's more, we can't afford it."

But I said, "The boy is desperate for work; he has three little sisters and a mother to support. What if we didn't help him and he turned to a life of thievin'?"

That did it. The boy was hired, and he fitted into the

Double Lazy Heart Ranch as neat as the last piece of puzzle fits into the pattern.

Charley's interest now switched from the ranch to the mustangs. He wanted to see that bill through. Each night when I came into the house—even before I dumped my groceries on the table and while the dogs were still yelping for joy—his eyes asked: "Have you heard?"

Then one morning the glad news came. Mr. Baring had presented our bill. It was a strong one, all right. Anyone using an airplane or a truck to capture wild horses could be fined $500 and sent to jail for six months. "A committee is studying it now, so it shouldn't be long, Annie"—that's how the letter ended.

Within the week there was a second letter, hand-written on three sheets of stationery. Alone at my desk I read it all through, and over again. But there was only one line that mattered, making my world all gray and bleak. "Congress has adjourned," it said. "Our bill never got out of committee."

I dreaded breaking the news to Charley, but he took it without flinching. "Why, Annie! My dear Annie!" he said. "You're not going to give up now, are you? The goal's in sight! Walt Baring will just present the bill again next session."

I swallowed hard and listened. Charley seemed as excited as a coach on a winning team. "You've got just a few months," he prodded, "before Congress meets again. In that time, you've got to prove to the world that compassion is mightier than money. You can do it, Annie."

"Maybe *we* can do it, Charley, but it'll mean giving up our weekend children."

Without hesitation he agreed. "They'd be the first to understand." And that's how we dropped another hard job for Charley, and that's how I had the time and the courage to begin all over again.

All this while we had depended on grownups for help. But now we turned to boys and girls. Year after year they had been winning blue ribbons with mustangs and half-mustangs at horse shows and county fairs. This was their war as much as mine. Why hadn't we thought of them before?

Charley made a gay stencil of wild horses high-tailing it for the hills, and this became my letterhead. Then to schools all over the country I wrote:

"No matter where you live—in a crowded city in the east, or on a farm in the middle west, or in the wide-open spaces of the far west—I know you care what happens to our American wildlife. It belongs to all of us, to you, and to your children.

"I used to think," I went on to say, "that the horsemeat I fed my dogs came from old, old horses who were tired of living, or ones who'd been injured and mercifully shot. But now I know that most of it comes from free-running wild horses. You should know this too." And I told them what was happening to the wild horses, all the brutal facts of their murder. Then I ended with the plea: "It might be *your* letter to *your* Congressman that will help save the mustangs."

Charley and I had no idea of the power of children's anger. Once they became aware of the cruel roundups their hackles rose, and they did something about it.

The way I heard it later, three little girls, still wearing their riding breeches, showed up at the home of Congressman

James C. Wright down in Fort Worth, Texas. They had been all over the neighborhood getting names signed to a letter on which one of them had typed:

```
We are writing a letter to Mr. Wright, Kay's Daddy,
hoping that he can help DO SOMETHING about these
horses!!!!! If you would like to sign your name to
this paper, it will probably help save some of them
. . . maybe all of them! Imagine . . . making DOG
FOOD out of horses . . . even wild horses! We feed
the birds . . . the squirrels and the chipmunks
. . . to SAVE them! Let's see what we can do about
saving the beautiful wild HORSES!!!!!!!!
```

Geof Hammett

Bruce Hammett
Barbara Lee Hammett   *R Gene Good-*
Nancy H.   *sell.*
Mrs Lennahan   *Mary Allgaier*
M. N. Bang
Mrs R. J. Baker   *I wish*
                           they   *ay*
                           would *WRIGHT*
Mrs Robert Soham   *stop*
Mr Shey J. Mathes
Mrs C.H. Lawrence   *Ginger Wright*
Charles H. Lawrence   *E. Allgaier*
Mr. J. H. Martin
Conway Douglass Weller
Helen Allgaier

I could just picture the scene that night. There he was: that tall, red-haired, bushy-browed Jim Wright, pacing up and down in his library, trying to unravel all the knotty problems in his mind. What to do about taxes, how to vote on foreign aid, how about Russia, how much more money should the government invest in getting a man to the moon, and how about his weekly *Newsletter?* He had to get that out, too. The thousands of people who had elected him always expected it. He was striding out his thoughts, sentence by sentence, and at the same time fingering a sheaf of notes he had made.

Jim Wright suddenly tossed all the notes into the waste basket and, grabbing the petition in one hand, he sat down at his desk and thrashed out his feelings into his dictaphone. Somebody sent me a copy of what he shouted, and this was it.

Any Congressman is likely to receive a petition every now and then, but this week I got one which really struck home. Among the signatures appeared some familiar names, those of my daughters, Ginger and Kay. The petition was the idea of two of their playmates. By the time it reached me it had the names of practically all the kids in the neighborhood and a goodly smattering of their parents.

It seems that some crass and thoughtless men have been cruelly mistreating a species dear to the hearts of childhood—horses. Out West, prof- iteers have been rounding up the dwindling herds of mustangs, peppering them with buckshot, running them to exhaustion with trucks and planes, and delivering them to the rendering plants, where they are sold by the pound and slaughtered for cat food.

My colleague, Walter Baring of Nevada, has introduced a bill to make it unlawful to hunt

wild horses on Federal lands with trucks or
aircraft. He is supported by a rancher's wife,
and by the kids of the nation.

These youngsters are in dead earnest. A fierce
purposefulness showed in their eyes as they
presented me their petition. This is no light
matter with them.

Am I going to be susceptible to pressure? Am
I going to be influenced by a bunch of children?
Am I going to support this bill because kids—
mine and others—are sentimental about the
wild horses? <u>You</u> <u>bet</u> <u>your</u> <u>cowboy</u> <u>boots</u> <u>I</u> <u>am</u>!

That same week a lanky thirteen-year-old boy stepped up
to the front of his seventh grade classroom in Ottumwa, Iowa.
Even with a broken collarbone from a fall off his horse, he
wanted to help the mustangs. His voice cracked slightly as he
said, "I make a motion that we have everything but the ice
cream at our class picnic and that we send our ice cream
money to Wild Horse Annie for her campaign."

The donation came, in dimes sticky with pink frosting
and chocolate cake. With it Charley bought pages of stamps,
the pretty ones with a flag on them, to stick onto *more* letters
to *more* children, asking them to write to *more* Congressmen.

With the flood of mail going out and coming in, Charley's
and my days were brimful. And we were strangely happy,
giving ourselves completely to the cause, and shutting the
door on our own personal worry.

20. A Growing Storm

I T WAS the boys and girls who helped us most. They were weaving a web back and forth across the land, touching many people, pulling them together. They were the ones who aroused the nation and turned the tide.

Help began coming in from everywhere. A big California paper, *The Sacramento Bee,* printed the boys' and girls' letters and headlined its own opinion of the ruthless slaughter:

DESERT HORSES FACE EXTINCTION BY HUNTERS!

Spattered across the page were gruesome pictures; they made me live all over again that terror-filled morning at Black Rock Desert. When I saw that the story was written by Al Trivelpiece, I almost wept. He was the one in Carson City who had chanted: "Here comes Wild Horse Annie!" He called me that in the article, too, but now he made it seem a badge of glory.

The voices of protest were growing louder just when we needed them most. Mr. Baring had presented his bill again. It had a number now—HR 2725. I sang it over and over as I swept our floors, as I peeled potatoes and ironed Charley's shirts, as I brushed Hobo, as I drove to Reno; it was like a secret code that could spring a trap and set the wild things free.

Al Trivelpiece's fiery story scorched a path all the way across America. The *Reader's Digest* noticed it. They sent a famous reporter, Robert O'Brien, out from Connecticut to see what the ruckus was about, to see if the mustangs were worth saving.

He chartered a little Piper Cub from a Wyoming rancher, Chug Utter, and the two of them flew over our crinkled ranges, trying to find some wild horses.

"Why, there's room enough here for millions of mustangs!" O'Brien said as he looked down on lava spillways, and brown treeless hills, and mountains scarred with landslides. From sky-high there was no life at all. Only mountains, tipped and tumbling. Only tiny, tiny trails no wider than thread. O'Brien kept his eyes glued on them, knowing that hoofs of vagabond animals had long ago carved them out, flinty hoofs of mountain goats—or maybe generations of wild horses in search of browse, in search of water. But now he saw no moving things.

"Looks dead as a moonscape!" he muttered.

Chug caught the boredom in his voice. "Here, you take

over!" he said. "I'll do the navigatin'. Keep your nose on the horizon and bear left."

Minutes went by. And more minutes. The needle of the gas gauge was getting close to the red.

"We'd better be heading for home," Chug warned.

Just then, far far below, there was a whisker of motion. O'Brien cut his speed and began a slow descent. He skimmed toward the movement. It was only a tiny whirl of dust. But all of a sudden the roar of his engine set the dust into motion. And blossoming out of it—*horses!* A whole string of horses!

"You take over!" he yelled to his partner. "I've got to see this!"

Chug gunned the engine, went into a spiral to hold altitude, then eased the ship fifty feet down, a hundred feet down. He was flying alongside the mountain now, parallel to the horses.

"Thirteen head! Three colts!" O'Brien was getting his story, shouting it. "It's the mares in the lead!"

"Sure, you big dude!" Chug shouted back. He reduced speed, lost more altitude, and the engine backfired. The horses reared up like rockets. The stallion, pure white, sprang into action, prodding his family, nipping rumps right and left. Faster and faster they fled toward the brink of a canyon. Toward self-destruction. They were going to dive!

"Bank away!" O'Brien shouted.

With a surge of power the plane banked steeply off to the east and left the wild horses blowing in fright, but safe.

On his way back home, O'Brien wrote down the end of

his story: "You never see these proud animals from the high-way any more. They never come down from the hills unless driven by planes. As my pilot and I watched the band moving swiftly across a mesa, he let out a shout of joy: 'More power to them!' And I say more power to Wild Horse Annie and her friends who are trying to save them."

The power came like a growing storm—from the corners of the earth a deluge of mail! The postman could no longer use the slit in the office door. He had to come inside and spill the mail on a table. Some of it was addressed just to Wild Horse Annie, Nevada. No city. No street.

Mr. Harris took the flood good-naturedly. He rubbed his fringe of hair in puzzlement. "Great guns, Annie! You're getting more mail than I am. You'll have to be a secretary's secretary to get it all read, let alone answered."

It was all I could do not to peek at my mail during work hours, especially at the ones with the strange stamps from faraway lands and the musty smell of travel about them. There was the big reddish stamp of Japan, with the lake and the twin mountain peaks with clouds dancing above them. And one from Australia with a Koala bear clinging to a eucalyptus tree, and a dancing girl from the Republic of Indonesia, and a bright plumed bird from Ghana. Sharp at five I swooped them all up and hurried home.

Charley, like Mark Twain, was a meat and potato man. But now, with all the excitement of the letters, supper was something to get over with in a hurry. Often he had the batter ready for buttermilk pancakes, or a chicken stew simmering on the back of the stove so we could eat right away. Then while I "redded up" the kitchen, he rummaged through the mail, happy as a squirrel hunting nuts.

"Listen to this, Annie! And this!" And he'd read aloud choice kernels from here and there. Some of them were written in a language so foreign we could not even read, except for the one word that was always spelled out in English. It was "mustangs." There was something about these letters that brought a tingling to the skin. Maybe it was the anger in them.

Charley carefully sorted them into neat little stacks—from children, from teachers, from ranchers, humane societies, businessmen, big and little. Always it was the children's letters we answered first.

We laughed a lot those evenings. One of our dogs, a fringy tan cocker, loved the taste of glue and we taught him to lick our stamps. Sometimes he even licked the flaps of our envelopes for us. He'd sit up, begging to get his licks in.

I loved these evenings, both because I felt good about our work and because they made Charley happy. And when he was happy, it was like wearing rainbows round my shoulders.

By the hundreds people wrote; by the hundreds we answered. In Portugal, an angry man, horse breeder and author both, gathered up a complete set of his works on horse training and shipped them to us by air. "Here's proof," he said, "that mustangs are a breed and can be trained for work or pleasure. Don't destroy that pure Andalusian blood!"

From Cyprus, a sergeant in a regiment of Scottish Highlanders exploded: "Fight back, Mustang Annie! Keep your elbow up!"

An old Indian chieftain, thin as a crow quill, sent us his picture with fighting words below it: "Let me at them two-legged skunks of wild-horse chasers with a band of my Sioux warriors . . ."

In New Jersey, a blind man ran his fingertips along the dots on his Braille copy of *Current News*. He pulled his stylus from his pocket and punched out his plea: "The fading drumbeat of wild horse hoofs that once pounded the western plains must not stop. What music they made!"

Up in Ladysmith, Wisconsin, Sister Mary Bridget was putting her light blue coverall apron over her black habit. It was very early morning but Brother Francis, a shaggy black burro, was braying his lungs out. He wanted his breakfast, and then to work in the little garden patch of the convent. As Sister Mary Bridget buckled on his halter and fastened his lead rope, she was thinking of the bill to protect wild horses. She was glad it included burros too. For Brother Francis' sake, and for all wild burros and horses, she wanted to help. So she wrote to her Congressman, and he drew up his own bill to protect the mustangs and stirred his whole state to action.

From all walks of life more and more letters came, and more mustanging pictures to back up my own. Each letter ended, "How can I help?"

"Write to your Congressman!" I urged. "Ask your friends to write, too. Let's unite in outrage, unite as Americans until

the lawmakers are swamped with a sea of mail."

The storm was reaching its peak. "Congressmen have never had so much mail over any one bill," Mr. Baring wrote. "They've been hiring extra help to handle it. 'Who's this Wild Horse Annie?' they ask. 'Does she know everybody?'"

Mr. Baring's letter ended on a sobering note. "We've done all we can. The bill has been assigned to a committee for study. There is nothing we can do now but wait."

Nothing but the waiting.

21. No Compromise!

GRANDMA ALWAYS said, "Time's got a lot of elastic to it. The way you feel inside makes all the difference. It's like one of those fat rubber bands. If you're havin' fun it's got no give at all, goes fast as light. But if you're waitin' on somethin' or somebody, it stretches till doomsday."

Now my restless waiting made me think of Grandma. How right she was! That monster Time was stretching out to the breaking point. Why was the committee wasting so many days? Why were they so slow? What was there to study? The mustangs couldn't wait. Nor Charley either. I could hear his breathing at night. It kept me awake, counting his three quick breaths to my one. I wanted so terribly for him to feel that he'd accomplished something important.

If only I could be down in Washington, fighting, instead of letting others fight for me. If only Washington weren't so far away: thousands of miles away, hundreds of dollars away. *If only . . . if only . . .*

Then all of a sudden one morning, Washington came to the office, to me!

"Could we see the person known as Wild Horse Annie?" a strange eastern voice said. "I'm from headquarters, the Bureau of Land Management, Washington." It was the kind of deep-timbered voice that comes through whatever you're doing. I couldn't hear what Ruthie answered, even though her reception desk was only a horse-stride from mine.

In a moment she was ushering two men over to me. One I recognized at once. It was Mr. Duck Fuzz from the Bureau office here in Reno. He gave me a sheepish smile. The other man was slick as a cedar waxwing. He wore a brown silk suit and carried a brown attaché case to match. He flicked a card out of his pocket and presented it with a bow.

MR. RAOUL REYNARD
Bureau of Land Management
U.S. DEPARTMENT OF THE INTERIOR
WASHINGTON, D.C.

Mr. Harris happened by just then on his way out to lunch. Nervously I introduced my callers.

"Annie," he said, "why don't you take these gentlemen into the conference room where you can talk in privacy?"

This suited me fine because our conference room was an exciting place. Instead of the walls being crowded with a lot of maps, jabbed with colored pins, they were alive with horse pictures. If Mr. Harris had ever told me to take one home for keeps, I'd have had a hard time deciding. There was a pony-express boy riding hell bent for leather with an arrow sizzling over his head. And a stagecoach pulled by six runaway horses, nostrils showing blood-red and manes and tails whiffling in the wind. There was a quieter picture, too, of an old gray mare asleep on three legs. But I guess my favorite was a copy of the mustang picture I first saw at the hospital. Yes, I am sure it was, even though it brought up times I didn't care to remember.

"These wild horses," Mr. Reynard said, pointing a mani-cured hand at my beloved picture, "are not the sorry-looking scrubs I've seen."

"No," I answered. "This picture was painted long ago, before planes and trucks forced the mustangs back into the hills where they almost starve." I thought my being direct like that would steer the men right to the point of their visit. But no, they had to skirt all around it, talking about the weather—how the days might be hot in Reno but so dry you didn't feel it, very different from Washington—and how lucky we were to have a fine office overlooking the beautiful Truckee.

"Yes," I said, "it's pretty now, but you should be here when it overflows every few years and swishes right through our office. All our files have to be put on dollies and moved." I didn't mean to sound impolite; I was just anxious to get on. But nothing could hurry them.

When they couldn't think of any more to talk about, they took a second look at the horse prints and then we all sat down at the big mahogany table.

At last Mr. Reynard cleared his throat. *"Harrumph.* Now about that mustang bill . . ."

He paused and a lump of fear began to form in my throat.

"My colleague and I," he continued, "agree heartily that any cruel planing of the wild horses must be stopped."

I sat forward, listening.

"And we plan to support your bill to the hilt. To the hilt!" he repeated, nodding his head vigorously with never a hair sliding out of place.

Tears of relief filled my eyes; I was afraid they were going to spill over. If Headquarters in Washington felt like this, the bill was as good as passed. I tried to smile my gratitude.

"There are a few words, however," he said in a confiding tone, "that we should like to add. As a reasonable person, you will agree to them, I am sure."

"Yes?" I asked, looking away and blowing my nose.

"You know what Mr. Baring's bill says."

Did I know! It was carved in my mind like the Ten Commandments.

"It prohibits," he began quoting, "the use of aircraft or motor vehicles in hunting any wild unbranded horse, mare, colt, or burro running at large on public land."

He paused to take a breath. I could hear my phone ringing and someone answering. Uneasily I wondered if it was Mom or Charley. "Yes, yes, I know," I said impatiently, "but what needs to be added?"

"*Harrumph.* Just strike out the period at the end, substitute a comma, and add: 'Provided that the Bureau of Land Management may authorize such activities in carrying out its duties.'" He adjusted the handkerchief in his pocket, and waited for me to speak.

"Mr. Reynard!" I gasped. "That would kill the whole bill!"

"Now, now, Miss Annie, you don't understand. I'm afraid I've not made myself clear. You see, we would employ only reliable pilots, and everything would be under the careful supervision of our BUREAU." He said the word in enormous capital letters.

I stared at the man. "I do understand." I tried to swallow my anger. "But so few mustangs are left! They're no longer a threat to the ranges."

"You're right, Miss Annie—that is, for now. You see, we do agree in all major points. But if the time should come when the wild horses multiply and overrun the ranges, the government must use airplanes to get rid of them."

Mr. Duck Fuzz put in his word here. "May I add, sir, that air pursuit is the least expensive and the most humane method."

I wanted to cry out, but I spoke quietly: "That could be true, *if* the horses are not sold to the rendering works. Those people don't care about rope burns, or even broken legs."

I grew bolder. "Do you have pilots in the Bureau," I asked, "that are trained especially for this work?"

Mr. Duck Fuzz reddened. He glanced unhappily at Mr. Reynard.

"No, we do not," the man from Washington admitted.

"Then you'd be using local pilots, wouldn't you?" I had to get at the truth.

"Probably we would."

"You'd need flying cowboys who know how a horse thinks, wouldn't you?" I persisted.

Mr. Reynard looked annoyed. But he remained polite. "I must say, Miss Annie, you've a sound business head on those slight shoulders. Your Mr. Harris is very fortunate indeed."

The compliment went over my head and out the window. Sharply aware now, I knew in a cold flash that he wasn't thinking of the suffering of the horses at all. And he would be using the very same roundup men I'd seen, men who could keep a horse just alive enough to walk into a slaughterhouse under its own power.

The man went on unruffled. "Now if you'll agree to the slight change, we'll give you a helping hand in Washington to put your bill through."

I made no answer.

"But if you don't," the voice never raised its pitch, "I must warn you that we'll do everything possible to defeat it."

I stood up, feeling utterly alone. And suddenly not alone. I remembered the child in the plaster cast, and her crying in the night from helplessness. And I remembered all of the helpless things of the earth crying somewhere in the night. And courage was there beside me.

The men were waiting for my answer. Mr. Reynard's mouth smiled a little, as if sure of victory.

I made my decision. "Your coming to see me is a great compliment," I said. "And I can appreciate your problems of range management . . ."

"Then you agree?"

"No," I said in a voice so cool I hardly knew it for my own. "The bill must stand as it is."

Mr. Reynard slowly picked up his straw hat and the brown attaché case. "I'm sorry to hear that," he said. "It forces us to oppose your bill." He held out his hand and limply, formally, shook mine. It was not a handclasp like Pa's.

I saw the men to the door, as Mr. Harris had taught me, and said good-bye. Then I noticed Ruthie waving at me madly.

"Quick, Annie! Get to your phone. It's long distance from Washington."

22. A Call from Washington

THE WAY Ruthie was waving at me, I thought it must be the President of the United States on the wire. But it was a woman's voice. Warm. Friendly. "Annie Johnston?" she asked.

"Yes," I said, still shaken by my talk with the Bureau men.

"I know all about your crusade for the wild horses, but you don't know me."

I could think of nothing bright to say, so I just said, "Oh."

"My name is Mary Warren, and I'm a director of the Society for Animal Protective Legislation."

Inside myself I repeated, "Society for Animal Protection!" I said a quick prayer. Dear God, please don't let it be chicks and bunnies; let it be the mustangs!

"Hello . . . hello . . . are you there?"

"Yes," I said with a little clutch of dread.

"I'm just calling to make sure you'll be here in Washington next Wednesday. You will, won't you?"

"Oh, no," I said quickly.

The faraway voice was plainly shocked. "But the sixteen members of the judiciary committee are hearing your bill then. The battle could be won or lost that day."

"I know."

"But, my dear, we understand you have facts and figures and pictures, too, that you could present."

"I do, but I hadn't planned to go to Washington. Mr. Baring has all the information. Thirty-two pages of it!"

There was a stunned silence. Then a sudden burst. "Why, you've been fighting to save the mustangs for years. And now when you're most needed you're not even coming to help?"

"No," I said thickly.

"Don't you care any more?"

"Care!" I choked on the word.

"Well, then, do you mind telling me why you are not coming?"

I had no voice at all.

"Is it because your employer won't let you?"

"Oh, no."

"Then what is it? Can't you please tell me?"

I thought, why not admit the truth? Why not? I almost laughed my relief. "We just don't have the money," I said.

Mrs. Warren seemed glad with relief, too. "Well, then, it's all settled," she said brightly. "The Society will take care of your expenses. Proudly!"

And before I could say yes, no, or thank you, she had thanked *me* and hung up.

All at once I was terrified. The nation's capital! Lawmakers by the dozen. Big bureaucrats. Big cattlemen and sheepmen. All fighting me, accusing the mustang. Accusing *me*. I had to get home to Charley. He could call Mrs. Warren, tell her I was sick, tell her anything.

"I just can't go!" I said when he had pried every word of the telephone conversation out of me. "I simply can't!"

Charley was standing in front of me, Nip and Tucker on either side, gazing up at him. "Why can't you, Annie?" he asked quietly.

"Because—because—if you must know," I sobbed, "I'm afraid. I'm plain scairt!"

He stood there, silent and thoughtful a moment. "Of course you are, Annie," he said gently. "We're all plain scairt of a lot of things. But fear is bad only when you're afraid of it. Actually fear breeds a special kind of courage. You might say a double helping. It makes you find the courage to beat down the fear; and the courage to keep on fighting."

Oh, my blind eyes. Here I was talking to Charley about being afraid, forgetting that he was fighting his dreadful sickness with all of the brave strength of himself, in silence.

I bit my lip to keep from crying; and Charley looked at me, smiling his understanding. "Now then," he said softly, "what do we do to get you ready?"

My insides were still crumpling. "I don't want to go without you," I whispered. Especially *now*, I cried to myself.

Charley shook his head as if I were very young and very foolish. "Who ever heard of a rancher going off in the middle of July? Even one who does have a hired hand? Besides," he added earnestly, "I want to see this bill passed as much as I ever wanted anything in my life. I couldn't do it in a thousand years. But you can! It'll be a living monument to all the Annies and Charleys in the world."

That settled it. Nothing could stop me now. Charley and twenty thousand mustangs were driving me to Washington.

Then panic set in again. I had only four days to get ready! Only four days to rehearse my part! How could I make the committee see and feel the cruelty of the air roundups? How could I make them care enough to do something about it? A sudden idea startled me. Why not make up a book for each member of the committee so they'd all be with me as I talked, watching just the way I did at Black Rock Desert?

Charley's eyes lit with enthusiasm at the idea. He went to work with a will, glad to have The Cause big inside him again. In Reno he found some notebooks, just the right size, with hard covers of blue buckram, and he bought India ink to make big black lettering, and he wheedled a photographer into making dozens of prints at cost.

Mr. Harris wanted to help, too. He insisted I do my mimeographing at the office, on his time. It was good to work hard again, pounding out stencils, cranking the machine, assembling the sheets.

Advice came pouring in, free. Say this! Say that! Suggestions piled up. Why not ride into Washington in full cowboy rig—chaps and boots and spurs and a big hat tilted on the back of your head?

"I'll think it over," I said, but Mom made other plans. She and Pa spent Saturday and Sunday at the Double Lazy Heart. Pa gave Charley a hand with the baling, so he wouldn't have to breathe all that dust, and Mom made me a blue linen dress, summery and blue as a Nevada sky.

Mom and I had a wonderful time, chattering to the whizzing tune of the sewing machine. Mostly, it was fast-as-lightning talk. But in the middle of a seam Mom took her foot off the pedal and faced me squarely.

"Annie," she said, clearing her throat and moistening her

lips, "I never been one to look up my family tree, because how do I know it wouldn't have a few wormy apples? But now I wisht I had, because my name being Clay, I wouldn't be a whit surprised if my forebears don't go right back to that famous Senator and horse-breeder, Henry Clay." She paused, shaking her head in sudden laughter. "Old Henry Clay," she continued, amusement and reverence all mixed up in her voice. "Cantankerous as a sour mule he was. But a bulldog kind of fighter for what he believed in."

I could tell Mom had more on her mind; so I just kept quiet while she finished the seam. Then she snipped off the thread and removed her glasses the better to see me.

"Remember, Annie," she said, "Henry Clay is the one who declared: *I'd rather be right than President*. So when you're up there on that rostrum, or wherever it is you'll be standin', just remember you are in the right. So speak out strong, for you're a Clay as well as a Bronn, and don't ever forget it!"

"I won't forget it, Mom."

The days were flying. Mrs. Warren had called on Thursday. Friday the mimeographing of my long speech. Saturday the sewing spree. And Sunday the notebooks readied—the pictures pasted in, just so, hand-in-hand with the words.

Came Monday, and you should have seen my desk! It was Christmas in July. Package piled on package. And underneath the tissue and bows were presents to make my head whirl. I felt royal . . . like a queen setting out to visit one of her colonies.

There was white cowhide luggage from Mrs. Harris, three pieces of it! And a purse with next month's salary from Mr. Harris. And a hat from the Junior Harrises; it was a little feather piece in white, small enough to sit on the back of my head, and I could pile my hair high in front of it, higher on one side than the other for that optical illusion; remember? And right there I tried it on, and the office boy let out a wolf whistle to brave me for the trip.

All this while Ruthie was standing in the most uncomfortable way, as though she had something to give too, but held back because of its smallness. At last, quite shyly she held up a pair of gloves, washed to snowy whiteness. "See if they fit, Annie. They're mine, but I want you to have them."

I pulled them on easily. "Why, Ruthie," I said, "they fit to a T. And I don't have any of my own."

It's funny how her little homey present made me cry when all the big ones didn't.

Tuesday. Good-byes. Out in the field early to say a word to Hobo. "I'll be back soon," I promised. "You take good care of the other horses. And oh, Hobo, watch over Charley while I'm gone."

Hobo wore hollows above his eyes now and his back swayed a bit with age, but he seemed all the dearer for that. He nudged me for a treat. I had a handful of shredded carrot to give and he lipped it into his mouth, chewing with slow measure, eyeing me all the while.

Unlike Hobo, Charley hated good-byes. I think he had planned to arrive at the airport just in time for my new luggage, heavy with the booklets, to get aboard. Mr. and Mrs. Slattery were there ahead of us with a box of candy, and the Governor's wife with a corsage. And Mom and Pa had brought me a scarf with wild horses leaping all over it. They seemed pleased when I tied it over my hat the way stewardesses do to keep their hair from blowing.

Charley had nothing for me, so I thought, and I was glad. It would have been more than I could bear. He and I walked out to the boarding ramp alone. There, with a quick motion, he tucked a tiny suede pouch into my hand. With a kiss he was gone. From my window seat I could see him climb into our old car, I could see him swing out of the parking lot and head toward home, to wait. My heart felt empty as a crater.

Carefully I laid the tiny pouch in my lap. I took off my scarf with the horses running all over it, and folded it into the pocket of my handbag. As the plane taxied to the runway and turned into the wind, I lost all sight of Charley. The captain was checking the engines now, one at a time, and the great plane sat there shuddering and roaring. Then another small turn and suddenly we were rushing down the runway and climbing to the sun. I looked down with homesickness upon the green Truckee Meadows melting away into the mountains.

Slowly I took off Ruthie's gloves and blew into them as Mom had taught me. "That way you make the fingers ready for the next wearing," she said. All this I did before picking up the little pouch and loosening the drawstring. Then almost timidly I slid my fingers inside and took out a slim, cool, piece of serpentine rock. It was striped horizontally in many colors—soft greens and yellows and grays and white. It was only about two inches long and shaped vaguely like a little horse, and it fit into the palm of my hand like a cool blessing. I held it a long time before I could read the note that came with it.

Dear Annie,

Meet Billii Bizhanee. He is a horse fetish that once belonged to the Navajos. To them the horse is ALL: their eyes, their legs, their heart. The old Indian brave who sold it to me said it belonged to a Medicine Man who carried it in a silver-studded bag along with his pollens, his shells, his bird feathers, and other magic things.

It is very old, Annie. Feel how smooth and worn it is. The Navajos believe it to be sacred because only mountains struck by sacred lightning produce veins of serpentine. They believe, too, that a spirit dwells inside to give supernatural power to its owner.

The Navajo word for horse is Billii; their word for luck is Bizhanee. So carry him in your purse, Annie dear, and rub him often for luck. Godspeed and Bizhanee to you, my little one.

Charley had forgotten to sign it, but I touched the place where his name should come. Then I refolded the note, tucked it away, and closed my eyes. With the little horse-figure still clutched in my hand I fell into a deep, untroubled sleep.

23. In the Witness Seat

IT'S FUNNY how you take pictures in your mind. You go into a strange room and come out remembering only one thing sharply—maybe a doll lying face down under a radiator, or a pot of pink-blooming violets in the sun. That's the way it was with me in Washington.

Mrs. Warren and Mr. Baring met me at the airport, and after a warm welcome, Mr. Baring said, "The newspaper people can't wait to meet you."

At my startled look, he put a gentle hand on my arm. "There's no need to be nervous, Annie. Newspeople are friendly folk. We'll go right to my office now."

When I walked in the door, Mr. Baring's words of assurance flew out the window. I expected to see three or four reporters, but there were so many they were standing and sitting double on chair-arms and window sills, and in my excited state they appeared to be hanging from the very ceiling. With scarcely time for a greeting, their questions came at me, thick and hard as hail. Yet afterward the only one I remembered was a lady reporter's asking how I managed to keep Ruthie's white gloves so clean!

But that evening when I read the newspapers up in my beautiful hotel room, my eyes opened in astonishment. All of the stories were lively and honest and full of fact. And between the lines you could feel the reporters' sympathy and outrage at the plight of the mustangs. I tore out the articles and had just finished a note to Charley when Mr. and Mrs. Baring whisked me off to a dinner party.

It was an elegant bib-and-tucker affair. Senators and Representatives were thick, and some as plump as raisins in a pudding. I remember how kind everyone was, calling me Annie as if we were old friends. But that's all I remember.

I lived that whole day-before-The-Day as if I were sleep-walking. I seemed to be two people. One of me was in Washington, in all the excitement and glitter. The other me was still in Nevada—running barefoot in the alfalfa fields, riding bareback in the wind; and I was still Charley's wife, sweeping our wide-board floors and washing dishes while I had all Heaven to look out on; and I was still Pa's Pardner—and oh, so homesick.

But next morning, the moment I entered the Judiciary Chamber, my two selves fused. I was one person: Wild Horse Annie on the warpath! No crusader marching to save the Holy Land could have felt his purpose more fiercely. Everything suddenly came into focus, sharp and clear. The room itself. Big. Cavernous. Darkly cool. The groups of sober talking men.

"We'll be sitting at the witness table right up front," Mr.

Baring whispered, trying to put encouragement into his voice. He was on one side of me and Tim Seward, his assistant, on the other, both holding an arm as if I needed crutches.

"You'll be the lead-off witness," Mr. Baring added.

"Witness?" The word brought me up sharply. This was a courtroom! I was on trial!

"Not you, silly!" It was Charley's voice, clear-sounding as though he were at my ear. "It's the mustangs. On trial for their lives. You're here to save them." Impulsively I reached into my purse and found my Billii Bizhanee. For the next two hours I held it very tightly.

"At that small table is the court reporter," Mr. Baring said, pushing my chair in behind me. "He'll take down everything that's said. And on either side, up front, are the newsmen."

"That many?" Down went my heart.

"Packed solid this morning, aren't they?" Tim Seward said.

I gulped. Then I saw three friendly, familiar blue notebooks on the table. Was it just two days ago that Charley and I had snipped and pasted them together? Or two years? Each had a little card with a name on it, like place cards at a party. Mr. Baring's copy was in front of him on my left, mine was in the middle, Mr. Seward's on my right. I resisted the temptation to peek inside. If I didn't know it all by heart now, I never would. I squinched my eyes tight shut. Without turning my head I could hear the murmur of the people coming in, filling the seats behind us.

"By jove, it's a full house!" Mr. Seward exclaimed. "Quite

a tribute to you, Annie." And in the same breath, "Look! The committee!"

My eyes flew open to see a file of sixteen men walk by. Some were middle-aged and paunchy, some young and eager. Solemnly they took their places around the table on the platform in front of us, and O miracles and wonders! That table —it was shaped like a horseshoe! I squeezed my Billii B. with a strong flicker of hope.

The shuffling sound of chairs and feet subsided. For a moment I was on a quiet island of thought. In the paneled recesses I fancied I could see shadow-figures of long ago, there to observe, perhaps, how it was all working out, this government of, by, and for the people, this dream they had dreamed.

"Mr. Chairman!" It was Mr. Baring's voice, and it had a resolute ring. "My bill before your committee this morning has as its purpose the outlawing of motorized and airborne roundups of wild horses and burros on all lands everywhere in the United States."

He paused for a breath and the meeting settled down.

"This bill," he went on, "was inspired by a young woman, the wife of Charles Johnston, who operates the Double Lazy Heart Ranch in Storey County, Nevada. Her courageous fight against the ruthless slaughter of the mustangs has earned her the name, Wild Horse Annie."

I felt eyes studying me to see if the name fit.

"But before listening to her testimony, let us pause. I believe that nothing in this country ought be done without prayer.

"God of Justice . . ." the surging roll of his voice reached into every corner.

I looked up, not meaning to, but gladdened to see a shaft of sunlight kindle the American flag above the chairman's head.

"We deplore man's inhumanity to man and beast. Without justice and fairness we are hopelessly lost. Help us, we pray, to deal justly in all things. In His name, Amen."

Heads slowly rose as the voice went on. "Members of the committee, the report of our witness is founded on first-hand evidence. She has twice risked her life to obtain this vital information. Gentlemen, I am proud to present my fellow-Nevadan, Annie Bronn Johnston!"

24. "We the People—"

A S I STOOD UP in the waiting quiet, Mr. Baring opened my notebook for me. He skipped the title page and the table of contents, and turned to page one so that I could read. But the only thing I wanted to read was the faces of the committee. Some were wide awake and alert, like track runners waiting for the gun. Some were relaxed and drowsy as if longing to finish out their morning's sleep. There were worried ones and wool-gathering ones, and a pipe-smoking thinker who put me in mind of Pa. I had to corral them all and lead them back in time and space.

"When Columbus discovered the New World," I began, surprised at how big my voice sounded, "he found no native horses. No wild ones. No tame ones. None at all."

Sixteen book-covers flapped open. Sixteen pairs of eyes looked down to read, then up to listen.

"The first horses to reach North America," I said, "were brought here in the early 1500's by a Spanish adventurer, Don Hernando Cortés."

At the mere mention of his name I saw him in my library book—in a tiny skirt like a ballet dancer, but the top of him in an armored vest, and his hair flowing black, and his eyes burning black, and his mustachios black. But I didn't mention all that; I wanted to keep everything bristling with facts. So I went on.

"His orders from the King of Spain were 'to sail the ocean-sea and conquer the New World.' He and his conquistadores were skilled horsemen and they easily took over the land, even though the native Indians outnumbered them a thousand to one. The Indians simply fled in terror, thinking each horse and man was one evil monster.

"*Horses were our Salvation,* Cortés sent word back to the King. *After God, to the horses belonged every victory.*"

The man with the pipe relit it and sat back in comfort.

"What kind of horses were they?" I asked, and suddenly I wanted to laugh out loud. Here I was treating this august body of Congressmen, some twice my age, as if they were my weekend children! But they seemed just as eager for the answer.

"To understand their breeding," I said, "we must go back to Arabia, to the Prophet Mohammed. A thousand years before Cortés was born, Mohammed had a vision. An angel commanded him to save the peoples of the world. So he summoned his tribesmen, and on their fiery little Arabian steeds they swept across the deserts of Asia and Africa, conquering tribe after tribe, along with all their horses.

"Nothing could stop them! Not even the Mediterranean. They rowed across it, horses and all, to invade Spain. It was a savage conquest, but some good came of it. The swift little Arabian and Barb horses were mated with the stout Spanish horses to produce a new breed, known as Andalusian. And it was this hardy Andalusian stock which Cortes, and later the missionaries, and later still the settlers, brought to America."

Everything in the room was quiet except for the stenotype machine, which made a clicking sound like the kind a beetle makes flying against a lighted window. The room seemed to contract. In all the world I was aware of only the committee and me. The committee bending over their books, turning the pages, and me reaching out to them.

"How did the Spanish horses get free?" I asked, warming to my own words. "It was the Indians who helped them! As soon as they overcame their fear, they saw what good buffalo hunters the Spanish horses would make. And so they lured them away from the missions and ranches.

"Of course, some horses sneaked away on their own, and stole away free. The New World seemed created just for them. It was a whole horse heaven of endless grass! Different from any they had known. They thrived on it, grew even tougher with their freedom, raised colts and grandcolts.

"In time their numbers swelled until the plains were flooded with horses. The sound of their hoofs was like the roaring of thunder in the mountains. From Mexico to Oregon more than five million were roaming free."

Sixteen pages rustled like the leaves of our cottonwood when the wind blows. I saw the next page in my mind, the word *mesteño* underlined in red ink. It was my cue.

"The Spaniards called those wild ones mesteños," I said, "meaning strayed or running free, but the English-speaking settlers changed it to mustang, a name as tough and hardy as the horse itself."

Right here I better tell you that my blue notebooks were quite thick—thirty-two pages, not counting the picture-pages. And I didn't intend to skip even one. I was here in Washington to do just what Mr. Baring had asked me to do: "Give the mustang's role in history, Annie," he'd said. "Present both sides of the picture—honestly."

Another thing I haven't mentioned is that all my life I'd had a secret longing for the stage. Maybe it was the blood of old Henry Clay stirring in my veins. Now the time had come! I must make my plea so strong, so fire-pure, that it'd be like lifting the committee by their lapels and shaking them into action. If Mr. Baring thought history was the key, now was the time to unlock the treasures of our little Washoe Library.

"Gentlemen," I said, "the tough little mustang has made American history. Lewis and Clark's expedition would have failed if it hadn't been for the mustang. They had rowed up the Missouri River until the mountains blocked them. Their trip might have ended right there, but the Shoshone Indians came to their rescue, willing to trade thirty mustangs. They were true-blooded Spanish horses; some even bore Spanish brands and had Spanish bits on their bridles. They carried the explorers and their tons of supplies and ammunition over the Rockies to the Columbia River. And so they saved Oregon and the Northwest for the United States."

The committee seemed pleased. They knew all about the Lewis and Clark expedition, but not the part the mustangs had played.

"And it was the mustangs," I said, "along with the oxen, that opened up the Santa Fé Trail. Through forest and desert, they blazed a path, leading the way for gold seekers and fur traders and for caravans of freight. This trail through the wilderness linked grazing lands to markets, and made possible the great cattle industry."

Several of the committee leaned forward in their chairs, as if this too was something new to them.

"And the famous explorer, Frémont," I said, "and his guide, Kit Carson, for whom our Carson City is named, used mustangs in their daring crossing of the Sierra Nevadas in deep winter. Only mustangs could have stood up to the blustery winds and blinding snow."

I was enjoying myself to the full. "And what horse, do you think," I asked, keeping my voice ladylike but strong, "what horse was used on the rough mountain end of the Pony Express? The little mustang, of course!"

My mouth was dry. I hated to waste time drinking while everyone was waiting, so I took just one sip to "wet my whistle," as Pa used to say.

Minute by minute the mustang's history was building up. "From the Spanish conquistadores, the mustang moved into the hands of the Indians, then to mountain men and trappers, cattle drovers and the stagecoach drivers, and the pioneer farmers. Saddled or harnessed, the mustang was the biggest one-horsepower in the world!"

I paused for a great gulp of air, and with a smile of encouragement from the chairman, plunged on.

"Gentlemen," I said, "didn't any of you have a grandmother or grandfather who told you of their little mustang teams that pulled their covered wagons across the desert and over the mountains to California?"

One man's eyes bridged the space between us with an electric spark. He must have had a grandmother almost as wonderful as my Grandma Bronn!

I didn't try to hide the joy I was feeling.

"So much for ancient history," I said and paused a moment. Somehow I felt that I was playing a role in history, too.

Up at the horseshoe table the men shifted in their chairs, uncrossed their legs, recrossed them, but without ever taking their eyes from the books in front of them. I could tell they were listening, just as surely as if they'd swiveled their ears like Hobo.

The man with the pipe seemed anxious to get on, to get right to the point. His face was asking: "What about those wild horses you want to save? Let's hear about *them*."

Looking directly at him, I replied, "With the opening of the cattle trails, more and more ranchers came west, bringing their herds of cows and sheep. They felt that every mouthful of grass was needed for their livestock, and that the bands of free-running wild horses were a big nuisance. So they took matters into their own hands. They killed the mustangs by the thousands. Only the fastest, the smartest, and most crafty ones got away and high-tailed it into the hills. The best survived to reproduce the species, which makes them all the more worth saving."

The pages turned, and the rapt attention urged me on.

"Today, enemies of the wild horse call him 'Broomtail' and point out that he's a far cry from the prancing steeds brought over by the Spanish conquistadores.

"It's true," I admitted, "that his royal blood has been diluted, but he still shows the spirit and courage of his Arabian ancestors."

It was funny how, for the first time in my life, I was talking and listening to someone else at the same time. "Tell the whole story. Be honest. Tell the *other* side, too." Mr. Baring was still prompting me from that day when he banged his fist on my desk.

I stood straighter, remembering.

"Because of the growing number of cattle and sheep," I said, "our government set up land management offices to protect the grazing lands. These offices have done a great service of conservation."

I was fighting and unafraid now. "The turning point came only recently with the big demand for canned horsemeat. This made killing the mustangs very profitable. Instead of just clearing the range to protect the livestock as before, wild-horse hunters could provide cheap meat for the slaughterhouses. The old technique of hard-riding cowboys was now far too slow. Speed and more speed was the cry, and so air roundups came into being."

Resolutely, I picked up my notebook and flicked it open to the roundup pictures. Even though the committeemen had their own, I made them look at mine, at me, so they'd know how serious it was, and how serious I was.

Making my arms into a music-stand, I held the book up before their eyes. Slowly I turned the pages, very slowly, my anger inheld.

"It's like a relay team," I said. "The planes drive the mustangs out of the hills, and then roaring trucks take up the chase. The horses often run fifty miles before they are caught."

I skipped none of the brutal practices. The ropes whanging through the air, choking their victims, the horses burdened with heavy tires, the cruel loading process, and finally the crushed cargo of rope-burned, bleeding horses.

The faces before me winced as if they themselves had witnessed the whole bloody business.

"Gentlemen," I said, "not one of us has any quarrel with the land management offices who protect our public lands. But we do object to the methods used in these roundups."

I was suddenly tired. I looked at my watch. I'd been talking nearly an hour! It was time to end. Quickly.

"Wide-scale range clearance is no longer needed," I concluded. "The mustangs are no longer a threat. They have been driven far back into the bare hills, and are living where it seems no horse should be able to endure. But they have endured.

"With so few left, it is time for us to protect them before they vanish forever. Only the federal government can do that."

Mr. Baring pulled out my chair, and I was glad to sit.

Mr. Lane, the chairman, rose to his feet and looked full at me. "You have given us an admirable presentation," he said. "Before we hear from the Bureau of Land Management, do I have your permission for a period of questioning?" His smile was friendly as sunlight on a summer hill. "We're not being argumentative," he explained. "We just want to understand everything very clearly before we make our recommendations."

I took a fresh grip on Billii B. and nodded my readiness.

"Gentlemen," Mr. Lane said, "you may put your questions directly to our witness."

There was a rain of questions, good clean rain that cleared the air. This was the best part!

The man with the pipe was first: "Since Nevada already has a law banning air roundups, why are you concerned about a federal law?"

"For two reasons," I replied quickly. "First, it is impossible to enforce our state law because it applies only to private land, and most of Nevada, you know, is in public domain.

"But an even bigger reason," I said, "is that the mustang doesn't belong just to Nevada. He is a symbol of freedom to all. He is our American heritage, as meaningful as the battlefield at Yorktown or the white church at Lexington. Even more so, because he is a *living* symbol."

From up and down the row the questions came.

"Would you want the Bureau to be denied the use of planes for scouting fires, spotting lost cattle and sheep, counting livestock?"

"Oh, no, sir. Planes are needed for patrolling the ranges. It is only when they fly low, right on the backs of the horses, that we suspect there is another purpose behind it. And this is the brutal practice that should be stopped."

"But, Miss Annie, if it ever does become necessary to clear the land again, are the mustangs of any value whatsoever, other than as pet food?"

"Oh, thank you for asking that!" I said. Now I could talk about *useful* mustangs! "Our Hobo is a mustang and he's almost thirty years old. My father owned him before I was born and worked him in his horse-and-wagon freighting business called The Mustang Express. Today Hobo is still my own special saddle horse. He has a ruggedness and a hardiness that none of our other horses have.

I couldn't stop myself. "And when my own father was a baby he was saved by the milk of a mustang."

Without thinking, it had blurted out. I could feel my face redden, but not one of the men laughed or even smiled. They just leaned forward a little so as not to miss what came next.

At this point a committee member who had remained silent handed a note to Mr. Lane, who nodded thoughtfully. "Suppose," he read aloud, "that the herds do increase so that they again become a threat to the ranchers. Do you propose no control at all?"

The question I needed! It opened the way for me to make my proposal. I wanted now to shout loud enough to reach President Eisenhower in his office in the White House. But in my quietest, most inheld voice I said, "Of course, your honor, the government must have the right to exercise controls. I'd like to suggest wildlife refuges where the mustang can roam free again—not just in Nevada, but in other states, too."

I could see heads nodding in agreement, but the man who had presented the question was puckering his eyebrows.

"If their numbers ever again become too great," I said directly to him, "the weeding out should be done humanely, with no torture at all."

The rain of questions beat on and the answers came dancing on the tip of my tongue. It was like a play that had been rehearsed a long time, and now the lines all fitted into place without any prompting. I was almost sorry when the chairman said, "This concludes our questioning."

Then he thanked me, thanked *me*, mind you, as a brave American. What was it Charley had said about fear inspiring a special kind of bravery? Maybe that was what he meant.

Then something happened which took all my poise away. Each member of the committee rose in turn and in a short speech paid tribute to the mustang's role in America and my part in protecting him. One boyish-looking Congressman, John Lindsay, said, "I have been told that this is the first time our witness has ever testified for or against anything. If this is her first time, I, for one, would never want to sit in judgment when she becomes an expert."

The laughter was warm and chuckly.

As I listened I made believe they were talking about someone else. And they were! That other Annie who had now burst her cocoon and was soaring.

Then the chairman stood up quite formally, almost at attention. I expected him to call on someone else, or perhaps to announce a recess, for it was already past noon. Instead, he stood with his head half bowed in my direction. And as though on one hinge, every committeeman, every reporter in the boxes, and my two beloved Nevadans stood at attention too. They looked so pleased and happy as if we were all part of something big in American history.

At last everyone sat down and a great hush fell over the room. The hush grew deeper and thicker until there was a mountain of silence.

"Curtain speech!" whispered Mr. Baring.

I felt my heart stop, then pound. It was easy to say fighting words, but I wasn't prepared for praise. I looked about at the lawmakers and felt little again, little as that lost baby field mouse.

Then all at once the warmest feeling washed over me. In the waiting stillness I could hear the liberty bell tolling, proclaiming liberty throughout the land, unto all the inhabitants. I could see mustangs running free. I could see a little buckskin colt with his mamma's milk still dribbling from his whiskers.

I felt overwhelming pride in just being alive. And pride in a country which allowed a little Nevada-nobody to stand up on its highest pedestal and speak her piece. At that moment I could have hugged Mr. Duck Fuzz himself. But what was I to say to these waiting people? An ordinary "thank you" to speak my bursting heart?

My mind was all in a whirl. Then, like soldiers marching, the images of men who had spoken for all of humanity began to walk through my mind toward one answer. And I could see the Plan as it had been from the beginning.

In the beginning was the word. The word was God. And God created man. And man was many things.

He was the grieving Abraham Lincoln at Gettysburg: *For us the living to be dedicated.*

He was the defiant Patrick Henry before the Revolutionary Congress: *Give me liberty or give me death.*

He was the young John Paul Jones, blackened by smoke from his burning ship and ordered to haul down his flag, who shouted: *I have just begun to fight.*

He was all the wise old heads who had framed a Constitution: *to form a more perfect union, to establish justice.*

And suddenly the answer was there. But I didn't know whether I could say it because my throat was all tight.

"We—*we the people*," I said, "have won." A tear started down my cheek, but I could see it didn't matter. The sunlight was streaming through a window, causing more tears than mine to glisten. We, the people, knew that we had won, and that we would always win so long as we fought hard enough for truth and freedom.

That was the Plan.

Roaming Free

AFTER the hushed stillness of the Judiciary Chamber, the corridor outside became a buzz of talking and rejoicing. Annie was surrounded by admirers, and to her delight some of the most warmly sincere were the Bureau men.

But on that memorable July day all was not perfect happiness. Word came from Nevada, through the foghorn voice of Zeke, that the canneries were stepping up their roundups to get all the horsemeat they could before a law would stop them. Chairman Lane and his sixteen men were told what was going on, and they acted swiftly, recommending to Congress that the bill be passed at once, without any amendment, and before the last bands of wild horses were wiped out.

Even with all the urgency, the evidence had to be studied again by the Senate. But the day came when Mr. Baring could wire:

Now only one more step was needed. It came on September 8, 1959, when President Eisenhower signed the bill into law. From that day on it became illegal for hunters to use planes for flushing wild horses out of the hills, or for trucks and jeeps to run them down.

The pen that the President used to sign the bill now hangs in a frame above Annie's desk. That is how she knows for sure that the long struggle wasn't just a wild dream.

Three years after the signing—in December of 1962— Annie and the mustangs received a wondrous Christmas present. The Department of the Interior created the first wild horse refuge in America. It is located on the high desert land of Nellis Air Force Base in Annie's home state of Nevada. Of the 3,000,000 acres belonging to the base, 435,000 now belong to the mustangs. Here they roam free in roadless, rugged country of juniper and pine and sage. Salt-lick stations have been placed near springs and waterholes, which the horses share with their fellow creatures—deer and antelope and bighorn sheep. There are no fences at all, only the faraway Kawich and Wheelbarrow mountains.

Most of the horses are a mixture of Spanish mustang, Indian pony, and runaway domestic horses. One, an Appaloosa stallion, is a splendid fellow with spots as round as polka dots. Already the rangers have dubbed him Chief-Thunder-Rolling-in-the-Mountains.

Annie, of course, was delighted with this refuge. But she had learned from firm, gentle Mr. Richards that the fight for freedom must never cease. When a second refuge was established in 1965 in the Cedar Mountains of Utah, Annie said, "That's good, but we need more—in Montana, Wyoming, Idaho; everywhere in the West. And why not?" she asked, the old fighting gleam in her eye. "We have the land and we have the descendants of the mustangs who helped us win it."

Time has robbed Annie of her wise and beloved father, who was saved by the milk of a mustang, and of her husband Charley, who made everything he touched seem beautiful. But Mom Bronn still parcels out her homely Clay-inspired wisdom. And she cooks for Annie, who is still Mr. Harris' secretary. She and Mom live in a little house on a hill with the spangly lights of Reno spilling out like jewels far below. Above, around, and behind them rise the mountains, craggy and bold. And somewhere in their rimrocks and mesas wild horses kick up their heels, magnificent in the freedom that is theirs because Annie and thousands of everyday people worked to safeguard it.

Autumn 1966

For their help the author is grateful to

WALTER S. BARING, U.S. Congressman from Nevada

MRS. JOE A. BRONN, Reno, Nevada

MR. and MRS. G. A. FREEMAN, JR., G—F Ranch, Capitan, New Mexico

EDWARD D. (*Tex*) GLADDING, Postmaster, Virginia City, Nevada

GORDON B. HARRIS, Reno, Nevada

MRS. CHARLES C. JOHNSTON ("*Wild Horse Annie*"), Reno, Nevada

ROBERT E. LOUGHEED, Newtown, Connecticut

T. W. MACAULAY, Cowboy and engineer, Reno, Nevada

DAVID C. MCCLURE, North Hollywood, California

WILLIAM L. MARKS, The Crystal, Virginia City, Nevada

SISTER MARY BRIDGET, O. S. M., Ladysmith, Wisconsin

GEORGE N. SAUM, Wayne, Illinois

GEORGE H. SEWARD, Assistant to Congressman Baring

JAMES SLATTERY, State Senator, Wadsworth, Nevada

AL TRIVELPIECE, Nevada City, California

LURA TULARSKI, Reno, Nevada

MRS. JOHN M. WOODARD, Sedona, Arizona

JAMES C. WRIGHT, U.S. Congressman from Texas

ABCDEFGHIJ